If you liked *My Royal Sin*, why not try

One Night Only by JC Harroway
No Strings by Cara Lockwood
Playing Dirty by Lauren Hawkeye

Discover more at millsandboon.co.uk

Riley Pine is the combined forces of contemporary romance writers as you them before. Expect delicious, dirty an swoons. To stay up to date with all thin head on over to rileypine.com for newsl details and more!

MY ROYAL SIN

RILEY PINE

MILLS & BOON

First Published in Great Britain 2018
by Mills & Boon, an imprint of HarperCollins*Publishers*
1 London Bridge Street, London, SE1 9GF

© 2018 Riley Pine

ISBN: 978-0-263-93221-8

MIX
Paper from
responsible sources
FSC™ C007454

This book is produced from independently certified FSC™ paper
to ensure responsible forest management.
For more information visit www.harpercollins.co.uk/green.

Printed and bound in Spain
by CPI, Barcelona

CHAPTER ONE

Benedict

MY KNEES ARE stiff against the cold flagstones. No surprise, seeing as I've been at prayer since before dawn. But my concentration breaks every time my gaze falls on the painting of the blonde angel, the one hanging above my head in the gilded frame. Instead of elevating my soul, she's become my secret torment, her innocent image taking center stage in my wicked fantasies.

Imagine if she were flesh and blood instead of oil and canvas. Better still…imagine those pouty red lips sheathing my shaft, her hot tongue taking me to heaven while I pump her greedy mouth.

During these brief daydreams, I'm not Brother Benedict, a holier-than-thou man in a white collar and black cassock. I'm just plain Benedict—a free man able to give himself to all perverted desires, damn the consequences.

I suppress a shudder. Freedom is the one possession I've never had in my privileged upbringing as the second son to the King of Edenvale.

It isn't only dangerous for me to lust, it's pointless.

Rising, I crush my fist into my prie-dieu. With a heavy grunt, I lean my weight into my split knuckles, leaving a small tattoo of blood on the polished mahogany, penance for my debauchery.

At that very moment, the rising sun hits my prayer room's stained glass window, and the pane glitters like so many jewels. I freeze, hypnotized as the multicolored shards cast reflections on my throbbing hand.

Hundreds of years ago, a long-forgotten artist had carefully selected each of these colors based on their symbolic meanings:

Red for courage and martyrdom.

Blue for heaven and the promise of eternal life.

Green for hope and victory over sin.

Gold for divinity.

White for purity.

I bow my head and retreat into the shadows, my stomach clenching like a fist, tight with guilt. I'm a seminarian and in one month's time I'm going to take my final vows for Holy Orders.

This is my duty. My life has been scripted for this moment since birth. I can't afford for my resolve to weaken.

I stride from my private prayer room to pace my austere apartment on the top level of a medieval watchtower that rises from beside the royal chapel at the edge of the palace grounds. From this vantage, I can see all the way to the river and to the north, the extensive manicured gardens of the castle, where my father, the King of Edenvale, resides along with my older brother, Prince Nikolai, and his new bride, Princess Kate.

A choking bitterness rises in my throat. I do not covet my beautiful new sister-in-law, but I do…covet.

Maybe it's pathetic to be turned on by a painted angel. But what can you expect from a twenty-seven-year-old virgin and almost-priest?

These days it feels like the Devil tests me at every corner, filling my waking hours with carnal urges. I am no saint, just another sinner.

And what's one more sin, to release the pressure in my thickened cock?

I make my way to my bathroom and flick on the shower, setting the dial to an arctic cold, and strip, maintaining eye contact with my reflection. My dark hair and arrogant nose reveal me as a member of the royal Lorentz family. My body is hard, but there is no pleasure to be derived from these cut muscles. They are products of long workouts designed to cleanse my mind.

The trouble is that nothing is working.

I step into the frigid spray and close my hand around my rigid shaft.

"Forgive me, Father," I mutter, beginning to stroke.

My actions are practiced. A firm squeeze at the root, twist at the head, grinding my palm against the crown. It doesn't take long until the bathroom fades and a fantasy takes shape. Today I'm grinding my cock between the soft orbs of a perfect ass, not penetrating the perfect rose-tinted pucker, but humping the silken crease. My imaginary lover offers a moan, pushing back her hips, urging me to quit toying and grant her release.

I slide my hand to her slick delicate folds and let out an agonized groan.

She tosses her thick mane of golden hair and regards me coyly over one shoulder. But her angelic eyes gleam a deep crimson red, alight with hellfire. Her wings extend and aren't white feathers, but ebony leather, and when she speaks, it is to promise to plague my soul for eternity.

My fantasies always end the same way. Troubled, to say the least.

My hand flies from my cock, and I fall to my knees, bracing myself on the tile. The shower spray pummels my slumped shoulders, but no baptism is on offer. Neither is physical relief.

In thirty days, I will stand before the high altar in the Shrine of St. Germain and fulfill the long tradition of my family entering the priesthood. My elder brother, Prince Nikolai, is the true heir of our people, and his recent nuptials mean—the Lord willing—that children won't be far behind.

For the good of the kingdom, I must step aside from the path to succession and consecrate my life to the cloth, as have all the second sons of our line. Once it becomes clear our seed isn't needed to propagate future kings and queens, we spares are quietly removed in order to prevent any family infighting.

And I am to do so with a smile on my face.

If I ever chafed at fate or held dreams to fall in love, to raise children, to have a life dictated by my own choices, those days are finished.

If I pray hard enough, if I purify myself enough, if I try harder…I will be the perfect priest.

Failure is not an option.

Our family has suffered enough in the years since our mother's unexpected death and it's a worthy fate, one that has the power to achieve so much good.

I need to suck it up.

Life could be a lot worse.

Rising, I flick off the water and towel myself off, my actions rough with self-loathing and disappointment. The harder I try to resist my urges, the more these lustful fantasies grow: orgies, BDSM, decadent and forbidden acts, signs that a burning desire smolders beneath my repression. I hate being a fraud, but I can overcome it.

Fire needs oxygen to blaze, and I refuse to entertain this behavior for a second longer.

Exiting into my bed chamber, I move with purpose back to my prayer room—and the gift from my elder brother—my golden angel. On the opposite wall of the gilded frame is a cedar chest, and inside is a black satin bag. I open the drawstring and remove the knotted leather whip. The towel slung around my hips drops, and I don't allow a moment's pause before grabbing the handle and bringing the cord between my shoulder blades with a biting blow.

Bright stars of pain explode behind my eyes. I recite the Lord's Prayer while continuing my self-flagellation, increasing the force of my swing as my gaze locks onto the angel's sorrowful eyes. She knows all, everything from my doubts to my hidden resentments about being the second son born into a mapped-out future. But I hope that she also sees my determination to bear the weight of family expectation.

After ten blows, my stomach churns and hot blood

runs down my skin. Good. Now I shall fast until sundown. The gnawing hunger should dull any unwelcome thoughts.

I'm fastening my white collar when a bell rings, a sign someone has entered the chapel.

A quick glance in the hall mirror provides confirmation that I appear every inch the picture of a serene priest eager to tend to my flock.

No hint of the devil within.

Ruby

I straighten my Cleopatra-style wig and dip my head to make sure the girls are in place, assessing the cleavage and how my breasts threaten to spill over the top of my corset. I take my chances that my client is a breast man, because, really, what man isn't? Clients tend to pay more when they salivate upon introduction. At least, that's what I've been told. In fact, I've heard some girls say they've taken home an evening's worth of pay from a man's ogling alone. But ogling won't be enough for this job. My instructions require far more than that, and though it's my first night of employ, I am required to give my client whatever he desires. And if he desires nothing, I must tempt him to want more. There is no work in this kingdom for an artist from a disgraced family, so I have to take what I can get. The Madam at The Jewel Box sought me out, and I couldn't refuse her offer, not when it meant I could provide not only for myself but also my brother's wife and child.

"They asked for Pearl, but I believe an ingenue will appeal so much more to our dear, inexperienced prince," the Madam had said before I left. "And you're the freshest of my pretty little blossoms. The flower not yet picked. Pearl's not desperate like you are. Plus, that damned bodyguard X would recognize her in an instant. I've been looking for a way inside the palace—and other buildings on the grounds—which means you get to be my little lookout."

"I don't understand," I told her. "You want me to spy for you? Why?"

I can still feel the sting of her palm against my cheek.

"And here I thought you'd been trained," she'd crooned. "Question me, and there will be consequences. Disobey me, and—consequences. All I need you to do is tell me if he owns a painting of an angel—until recently, one I was led to believe had been destroyed when your father passed—and report where the painting is." She smiled her mirthless smile, and I fought back tears at the mention of Papa—at the fear of being struck again. "Darling, you not only get to seduce a celibate prince, but you get to find me something very valuable. Succeed in gathering the prince's attention—and finding what I seek—and you'll be a jewel as prized as your name. Succeed, and you and your remaining family will want for nothing as long as you remain in my employ."

I swallow the threat of my own conscience trying to weigh in. What do I care about a stupid painting or what she wants with it? I have the chance to save my brother, Jasper. That's all that matters.

So I repeat her words over and over again to center myself in the moment—to remind myself of what I must do.

I nearly break an ankle climbing the chapel stairs in these boots, four-inch stilettos that cuff just below my short skirt. After almost two months of my apprenticeship, I'm used to the shoes and clothes, but my attire was not built for more than seduction.

There's also the small fact that I'm on the Edenvale Palace grounds—making my way to an apartment in the lonely-looking, ivy-covered tower next to the chapel. My phone rings, and instead of silencing it as I pull it from my pocket, I accidentally answer it.

"Hello? Are you there?"

"Shit," I whisper-shout as I scramble back down the steps. "Camille, I'm here. Just…give me a second…" I race outside and around the corner, through the first door I see, not wanting my client to catch me conducting any sort of personal business when I am supposed to be…working. Complaints equal a reduction in my take, and some, I've heard, suffer worse.

I freeze, though, when I realize where I am—in the Royal Edenvale Church itself.

"Is everything okay?" I whisper into the phone, and I hear my brother's wife sniffle before she speaks.

"You're…you're working. Aren't you?" Her voice breaks on that word, *working*, and I can hear her anguish, her guilt.

"Yes," I answer, trying to soothe her with the one word. "It's okay. Don't worry about me. But something is wrong with you. Tell me what it is."

She sniffles again. "I took Lola to visit her father today. It was the first time I brought her with me, the first time she would see Jasper in two months, and when the guards told him we were there, he refused to see us."

I suck in a breath, both at Camille's pain but also for my brother, Jasper. Because I'm at the Edenvale Palace, completely out of my depth, about to seduce a man I've never met—a prince, no less. I understand his shame.

"He loves Lola. You know that. And he loves you. But prison is no place for a child. And you can understand him not wanting her to see him like that. Can't you?"

I hear the clang of heavy shoes on metal in the tower entryway next door, which can mean only one thing. My client is approaching.

"He wouldn't refuse to see his child," Camille weeps. "Something is wrong. I can feel it in my bones."

"I'm sorry," I say frantically, trying not to let my own worry about Jasper sink in but also not wanting the prince to find me hiding out in the chapel on my phone. "I have to go, but if tonight plays out as it should, I will have enough to pay this month's lease on the cottage. You and Lola are safe for now. That is all that matters."

"But—"

The door from the stairwell starts to slide open, and because I have no choice, I end the call and sneak past the pews and into a confessional. I'm still trying to calm my breathing when the shadow of a man appears on the other side of the lattice.

"Have you come to make confession?" a deep, gravelly voice asks.

I stopped believing in any higher power long ago.

But I know why I'm here and what part I need to play. "Forgive me, Father. For I have sinned."

I open the screen on my phone that has my script for our introduction. I must believe in my brother's innocence, and that giving up my own will set him free. If I can earn the money the Madam is talking about, then I can buy the best legal representation and set my brother free. Jasper Vernazza is a world-famous art historian. He'd never dream of stealing anything from the museum to sell on the black market. Someone set him up, but for the life of me I cannot imagine why.

"You may proceed, child," he says. "The Lord is ready to forgive your sins."

I stroke a finger along the lattice grate and hum, reminding myself to play the part for which I'm being paid.

"What if I want to keep sinning?" My voice is breathy and soft as I infuse it with the need a client would ache to hear. It's practiced need on my part, of course. But if my training was a success, he won't know the difference. I glance at the screen in my palm. "What if all I want is to relieve you of that desire pulsing between your legs?"

"Who sent you?" he says, and I can tell he speaks between gritted teeth.

"Let me taste your thick, aching cock, Father," I say, my voice sweet as an angel as I try to sound less like I'm reading and more like this is what I truly want. "Let me take you so deep. I want to feel you throbbing, salty sweet against my tongue—"

I jump at the sound of what must be his fist thumping the wall between us.

"Who. Sent. You?" he interrupts, but I will not be deterred, not when my only choice is to succeed.

I scroll through the preplanned dialogue on the screen. "Think of all those times you've come alone," I tell him. "Every fantasy you've ever had, every sinful act you've dared to let yourself imagine—I can be that for you."

His breaths are ragged, but he does not speak.

I glance at the screen again as a text notification pops up, catching me off guard.

"'Why did you hang up on me?'" I read, but then realize I've read it aloud. And then I add, "Shit!"

He breathes in, and I can tell he's about to speak, so I fast-forward to the next step to regain control of the seduction, even if it is a lie.

I let go of the lattice and slip my free hand under my skirt, closing out the text and returning to my lines.

"Highness." I moan as I slip a finger beneath my thong, working myself until I'm wet. "Do you hear that?" I ask, plunging two fingers into my now slick heat. "That's my pussy, so ready for you. Don't you want a taste? Just a little lick?"

You need the money. Your brother's life—the lives of his family—depend on it.

This silent reminder plays on a loop in my head as I try to lose myself in self-pleasure before I get swallowed by regret.

This is for your family.

I swirl a slippery finger around my clit and gasp, the phone clattering to the floor. "Don't. You want. To make. Me. Come?" I ask between pants, the words all me now. I am lost in the moment just as if I were in the tiny bedroom of my old flat, taking myself to a place that is not here, in this church, but somewhere I am safe. Somewhere I am wanted rather than paid. "Is your hand on that cock, Highness? Is it daring you to bury yourself inside me? Because all you have to do is step into my side of the confessional and sheath yourself to the hilt."

I try to bring myself to climax, but even I can't forget entirely where I am or why I ended up here. So I embellish, crying out in feigned ecstasy.

"Oh… Your Highness. Oh God! Your Highness, I can't—" I add a few more gasps before yelling, "Benedict!"

"Enough!" he growls, and I collapse onto my knees with a satisfied grin.

Yes. That was quite enough.

He waited until he thought I was done, which means he didn't want me to stop. If that's all that comes of tonight, I have succeeded in the first step for which I have been hired.

You must earn his trust and break him.

Because this is not just any client on the other side of the wall. He is a prince, second in line to the throne and brother of our future king. I've just attempted to get myself off in the presence of a man I've only ever seen on a television screen or staring at me from the pages of a newspaper.

I let down my guard for mere seconds and scramble for my phone on the floor, which is why I startle to see him standing in the opening of my booth.

"Forgive me, Father," I say, straightening the skirt that barely covers what lies beneath. The air smells of sex, and the man looming before me stares with beautiful green eyes. "Did I make you sin?"

He grabs me by the wrist, and I paint on my most wicked grin.

"Come," he says and pulls me from the booth.

I force a playful laugh. "But, Your Highness…I already have."

CHAPTER TWO

Benedict

THE WOMAN FROM the confessional booth is sin in stilettos. Her angled bob accentuates her heart-shaped face, highlighting porcelain skin and perfect crimson-painted lips. While her mouth slants into a coy smile, eyes are said to be portals to the soul, and her violet-blue irises hint at secret pain.

"For the last time, who sent you?" I ask her gently, a wolf in lamb's clothing. Because her unexpected performance has had the desired effect. My cock strains against the thick band of my boxer briefs, where I clamped it securely in place before pulling her out into the light. The air around us is perfumed by a salty, rich tang, a scent not unlike my own release, and yet beguilingly unique.

Is this what women smell like between their legs?

A muscle in my jaw twitches even as my nostrils involuntarily flare. My mouth waters.

"Sent me, Your Highness?" Her lilt reveals she is from Rosegate, the disputed territory on our northern border with Nightgardin.

Interesting.

Rosegate whores are notorious throughout Europe, hothouse flowers offered to elite clients for the price of what most people make in a year. And I can see the appeal. If I wasn't planning on offering my inheritance to the church, I'd gladly use it to open this woman's petals, to press my tongue to her bloom and drink in her dew.

"What makes you think someone sent me?"

I bunch my hands into fists, will my lust into an internal dungeon and padlock the door. My duty is to provide this woman respite from whatever spiritual matters weigh on her soul.

Nothing else.

"You passed by no less than four guard posts, then over acres upon acres of landscaped ground covered in Europe's most state-of-the-art surveillance system. Yes, my child, someone indeed sent you to me." But who would want to tempt me from the righteous path? Was it a trick of some discontented servant?

"Oh please." She huffs a laugh but refuses to meet my gaze. "I'm no one's child."

She's right, of course, even as she evades my question. Her ripe body is pure woman, but she is younger than my own twenty-seven years. If I were a betting man, I'd wager she was at most twenty, a young woman who should be busy studying at university, not here at the royal chapel, being paid to seduce an almost-priest.

"You have two choices." I draw myself to my full six-foot-five-inch frame. "Either give up a name, or I'll be forced to take you upstairs for questioning." I don't exactly know what that entails, but she can't remain here in sight of Christ on the Cross. "Follow me."

"Are we going to your bedchamber?" She skims her hands over her breasts, the tops spilling over her tight outfit, the skin soft and succulent as a peach.

"Not a chance." I can't question this woman anywhere near my bed.

That leaves one option.

I begin walking, my pace fast and unfaltering. I might not be heir, but I took my first steps in the throne room and arrogance is my default. I was raised to lead, to expect others to follow. After a moment, the sharp clicks of her heels behind me confirm my assumption that she is keeping up.

We enter my personal tower and I lead her up the spiral staircase. "Do we have far to go?" she asks after the second floor. "These boots aren't made for walking."

I'll give her that, all right. They're made to draw the eye to the lush curve of her shapely thighs.

"In here," I say crisply as we stop in front of a carved oak door.

I open it, and the bright summer daylight shines dimly through the slitted windows, an architectural holdout from when medieval archers used these openings while stationed in the turret.

She scans the floor-to-ceiling bookshelves and gasps. "I've never seen so many books in one place except at the royal library."

I swallow a smile. My personal collection is rather extensive."

Little does she know that hidden behind covers like *A History of French Cathedral Gargoyles* are entirely different reading materials: *Story of O*, *The Joy of Sex*, plus a stash of Greek and Egyptian erotic art. Studying sexual arts is something of a twisted hobby. While I may be inexperienced, I'm far from ignorant in the ways of giving and taking pleasure.

"Sit." I gesture to a leather chair. It takes all my willpower not to revel in the length of her creamy thighs, exposed beneath her tiny skirt. I walk to an antique globe on a desk and give it a spin. "Were you sent by Nightgardin?"

Nightgardin is the kingdom to the north of our borders. Like Edenvale, it is small by modern standards, more a Luxembourg than France, but our mutual enmity has spanned centuries. For generations our two countries have warred through battles and of late, diplomacy, to control Rosegate, a much-admired city that sits on our border, claimed by both kingdoms.

Desperation darkens her gaze. "That's not important."

"I disagree. Nightgardin would take pleasure in exposing me as a hypocrite right before I take my holy vows."

"Please, believe me." Tears fill her eyes as her delectable bottom lip tremors. "I don't know anything. The Madam simply informed me of my assignment. A town car picked me up and brought me here."

My brow furrows at the anxiety in her voice.

"Crap." She covers her face with her hands. "I am blowing this so hard. Madam will fire me without a second thought, and I will be royally screwed. Please, Highness. Father. Whatever. Let me suck you, fuck you. You can have me anywhere, penetrate any place." She drops to her knees and tosses her hair back from her face.

"Anything?" Her offer warms my belly like a shot of scotch. "You'll let me act out any fantasy? No inch of you is off-limits?"

Her pupils widen, the delicate vein in her neck pounds. "I am yours to command."

Someone is hell-bent on sabotaging me. But the joke could be on them. Tonight's encounter could grant me a path to redemption that no one has counted on.

This woman offers me the chance to break every rule. But what if I can withstand her angelic body? Here is the perfect way for me to cast doubt aside and prove myself worthy of taking my final vows.

"Stand up. I have a proposition."

Ruby

I swallow hard. Whatever he proposes, it cannot be enough to sway me from my purpose. I must make him give in to his lust, make him trust me, or we will lose everything. I close my eyes and remind myself of the stories some of the other girls have told me, though these tales are nothing found in the books that line the library's walls. They claim it wasn't always like this, that the Madam had changed ever since she'd returned from a trip to Nightgardin a year ago. Now she punished her girls for losing a client— and let clients dole out whatever consequences they saw fit, as well.

I once lost a month's wages for not swallowing when my client came in my mouth.

I know a girl who had her nose broken for telling her client he needed to bathe more often.

One girl got caught by her client's wife. The Madam not only fired her but had them scar her face so no client would want her after that, just in case she tried to do business independent of The Jewel Box.

I don't want to know who *they* are or how they enact physical punishment, but the prince has not yet kicked me out, so I will humor him and listen to what he proposes.

"What do you want from me?" I ask. "I've already offered you everything I have to give."

Myself.

He walks along the shelves, running a finger over the spines of the books.

"I take my final vows in one month's time. If it is, in fact, my brother who has put you up to tempting me, then he shall get his wish. Just not as he thinks."

My brows furrow, and he turns to face me as he continues.

"This—" he points to his collar "—has always been my path. The eldest son will rule the kingdom, and the spare will keep the royal family and its subjects on a moral path. The third... Well, you've heard of my brother Damien's banishment. Our family has been disgraced enough. I will not add to it." He raises a brow. "I know the rumors about my mother."

My cheeks burn. Though the queen died many years ago, gossip of the second son—of the man standing before me—being a bastard has long circulated throughout the kingdom. The origin of his birth means nothing to me. All I care about is *my* duty. *My* family.

"For many reasons," he continues, "this is a responsibility I have never taken lightly. Until now I have not succumbed to the temptation of the flesh, but then, I've been careful not to let myself truly be tempted."

I rise to face him, but he still towers over me. "Stop speaking in code, Your Highness. I came here to do my job. Are you or are you not sending me home a failure?" I don't think the Madam truly cares whether I am able to seduce him or not. I just need to stay long enough to look around—to find the painting she's so convinced is on these grounds. I try to sound tough, not to let on what failure could mean, but the tremble in my voice betrays me.

He reaches a hand toward my face but squeezes it into a fist before his skin meets mine.

"Tempt me," he says, and a muscle in his jaw ticks.

"I don't understand," I tell him. "I thought I already tried."

He unfastens his collar and pulls it from beneath his shirt. "I am not worthy of the priesthood unless I truly can resist. Unless I am genuinely tempted. Whatever your fee is, I will triple it if you come here nightly to try to lead me from my virtue."

My breath catches. Triple my fee. Nightly. Surely the Madam will free me from my original obligation if he is willing to pay such a wage. And coming to him every night? Wouldn't that give me access and time to find what she seeks?

"Nightly? Would you send for me when wanted, or shall I show up and surprise you?" I laugh and bat my lashes at him. "Like tonight?"

He shakes his head. "If you need to do this to provide for yourself…" He nods at my attire, the small gesture filling me with more shame than masturbating in a confessional.

The Prince of Edenvale sees me as a whore. I have to remind myself that is exactly what I am now. Once upon a time, I was the beloved daughter of a famous and respected man. But I am not that girl anymore.

I raise my chin in a futile attempt at defiance. "What?" I ask. "Say whatever it is you were going to say next."

He runs a hand through his thick, dark hair, and I realize that whatever he's about to propose, he's nervous.

This realization melts a little of the ice around my heart.

"There is a cottage past the gardens in the center of the maze. It's been vacant for months, but there is staff assigned to clean and maintain it in case of visitors. It is ready for you right now."

My pride begs me to refuse him, but the thought of another night in the brothel has me putting logic, comfort and safety first.

"I can't afford rent," I say coolly.

"There would be none, of course."

"And during the day?" I ask.

He nods. "Your days are your own to do as you please, on or off the palace grounds. I will send for you nightly at eight o'clock. Our work begins tomorrow."

On or off the palace grounds.

I can find that painting in a matter of days.

"What other rules are there?" I ask, waiting for the catch, for the other shoe to drop.

He clasps his hands at his waist, the collar between them. "As long as your skin never touches mine in a sexual nature, there are no other rules. Do what you will to tempt me from my path."

He reaches a hand toward my face again, and just when I think he's about to break his own rule, he pulls my wig free, letting my blond waves tumble over my shoulders. Again that muscle tightens in his jaw, but he is otherwise unreadable.

"And never," he says, his voice gentle yet authoritative, "wear this again."

He wants to pay me triple what I'd make with any other clients—without him ever laying a hand on me. I swallow tears and extend a hand. "I'm Ruby." I give him my fake name from the brothel, and he hesitates, my wig in one hand, his collar in the other. "Shaking hands doesn't violate any rules, does it?"

The corner of his mouth quirks into something almost like a grin. Almost.

For a moment I'm tempted to tell him the truth. I am Evangeline Vernazza. Surely he would recognize my father's surname. But no. Prince Benedict and I are more similar than he thinks. I know family disgrace as much as he does. I am not a budding artist, daughter of a respected name anymore. I am Ruby, the newest escort from The Jewel Box, the most prized brothel in Europe.

He drops the wig to the floor and takes my hand. "It's nice to meet you, Ruby."

I smile enough for the both of us. "Your Highness, I'd say you've got yourself a deal."

CHAPTER THREE

Benedict

I HAVE NEVER laid eyes on this woman in my life, so why does a strange recognition thrum through me? Ruby's golden hair tumbles over her narrow shoulders, loose curls that skim the swell of her breasts as they rise and fall. Her unease is palpable, a problem when my own instincts are hardwired to provide comfort. I flick my gaze to the wall where a discreet intercom system blends into the sumptuous red-and-gold wallpaper. Never once have I summoned for the help of those who wait around the clock for my beck and call. But this woman is causing me to break all of my rules.

I cross the room, press and hold the small button. "X, I have need of you."

"Very good, sir." My bodyguard's response is cool, clipped and unsurprised. He had guarded my brother Nikolai for years but asked to be reassigned to me after my brother's engagement to his matchmaker, Kate. The request came as a surprise. X joked that he had grown tired of being surrounded by all

the newlywed romanticism. If that's true, he came
to the right place in heading up my security detail.

At least, until tonight.

He appears a moment later, seemingly conjured
from thin air. His suit is impeccably tailored, his
implacable features revealing no shred of shock to
find a seminarian alone with a scantily clad lady of
the night. Nor does his mouth so much as quirk at
my next order.

"This is Miss Ruby. Please escort her to the gardener's cottage within the maze and see to it the
quarters are well provisioned. It should go without
saying that I expect a high degree of discretion."

"Of course, Your Highness." He is the consummate professional. No hint of incredulity. No second glance at the young woman's thigh-high boots.

"Spare no expense on food, beverage, clothing.
Her wish is your command." I offer no further explanation. None is required. Being a prince of the
blood means never having to give a reason.

"Understood."

He turns and offers his arm. "Miss Ruby."

Her hand trembles as she accepts his gallant gesture.

"But what about my things at my...workplace?"
she asks. "I don't have much," she admits, and
I wince at the thought—at the excess in which I
was brought up—and suddenly I want to give this
stranger everything she lacks.

"I see." X's steely eyes hold a hint of a twinkle.
"Well, it just so happens that Monique Mantissa is
an old friend."

She gapes. "The designer Mantissa?"

He inclines his head. "I believe her fashion line is rather popular."

Ruby's laugh deepens, a husky melody that makes my skin sing. "Um, if by popular you mean appreciated by those who shop at Versace, Chanel or Prada. You know Monique Mantissa. She is rock-star famous. Her shoes are… There are no words." Her eyes take on a glow that I've seen only in nuns after a rapturous spiritual revelation.

The fact X knows such a person is of no surprise. He worked for years as my brother's personal bodyguard before his abrupt reassignment after Nikolai's nuptials. That reminds me.

"Also there is to be no mention of this arrangement to my brother or the king," I command.

"Not a word. Perhaps it would ease your mind to know your father has decided to expand his current travel to fly to New York for a United Nations summit, and Nikolai and Kate left for the Hawaiian Islands on honeymoon this morning."

"I see." If a man deserves happiness, it is my elder brother, who finally found true love in a most unlikely place, with the matchmaker assigned to find him a wife. I do not resent his position. His future crown has never been my ambition.

And yet…

And yet nothing.

I swallow hard, refusing to allow any of my true dreams to float to the surface.

"It appears that you have the run of the place. Will you need anything else, Highness?"

"That will be all," I snap, my tone gruffer than intended. "Wait. Take my Black Amex for the shopping spree. And, Miss Ruby, I shall see you in my bedchamber tomorrow evening when the sunset fades from the evening sky."

Her expression loses some of its innocent pleasure. After the sound of their footsteps fade, I return to my room, guilt eating at my stomach.

They don't exactly teach "Obliterating Sexual Urges 101" in the seminary. I am a man with a man's needs. But I'm also a prince, a second son, who has a duty. I can't let Father down. Especially when my face is the one that looks nothing like his. I was raised surrounded by the whispers that my mother, the queen, rest her immortal soul, grew lonely during a long absence from my father twenty-eight years ago and took comfort in the arms of the Captain of the Guard. A man some might say is my true father, except to voice such a claim in public would invite charges of treason.

But my blood runs with hidden lust, and in my heart I know that is my legacy. Born in sin, forged by an act of fornication. Father has never acted on these rumors, but he has always kept me at a kingly distance, his touch always a little cold, a little distant. To admit me a bastard would be to admit himself a cuckold.

So I am allowed the titles, the acceptance, the palace life.

Now it is time to pay the piper.

I fall to the unforgiving floor. "Oh, Lord, please grant me the strength to face this challenge."

Ruby

A knock sounds on the cottage door promptly at eight in the morning. I lie in the unfamiliar bed, blinking away the best night of sleep I've had in ages. I burrow further into my pillow, hoping I imagined the sound, and let out a blissful sigh.

I think I want to marry this pillow.

Knock. Knock. Knock. Knock.

This time it is loud and unmistakably real. I rise from the bed and wrap the sheet around my naked frame. I know it will not be Benedict. He said my days were my own. He will not require my…services until nightfall. Whoever dares to wake me at such an hour is not worth the time it would take to get dressed.

"I'm up. I'm up," I groan as I unlock the door only to find a young man dressed in what I assume is the attire of a palace servant—a black double-breasted tuxedo coat and tails, a vest and white bow tie. Wow. I wonder what they're required to sleep in if this is day wear.

"Miss Ruby," the man says, wheeling in a silver cart with covered plates on top of it. "X has requested you eat and dress so that you are ready to meet him at the palace gates at nine. A groundskeeper will pick you up in a golf cart just outside the maze in fifty-five minutes to bring you to the car."

After being told I was free to do as I choose, I open my mouth to protest. But that's when I smell the buttery sweetness of baked goods, the aroma of fresh coffee. My mouth waters, so I close it before speaking a word and swallow.

"What does Mr. X need me for at nine in the morning?" I ask.

The man uncovers a platter of scones and croissants, another of fresh fruit. He then pours coffee into a porcelain cup and bows his head.

"Shopping, miss. That is all I was told." He smiles softly. "And you may call him, simply, X."

My eyes widen as I remember X's mention of Monique Mantissa, of Benedict offering his credit card. I have never been the kind of girl to get worked up over material things, especially now that I must do whatever I can just to make ends meet not only for me but for my niece and my brother's wife. But I just slept in a bed fit for a queen and am about to eat a breakfast fit for a king. Is there anything wrong with living like a princess for a day?

To avoid the guilt that threatens to take away my moment of joy, I remind myself that this is all part of earning triple my fee, all of which I will use to support Camille and Lola. Camille's teacher's salary alone barely covers their rent, let alone the legal fees piling up since my brother's arrest. With this job, I may be able to hire a proper advocate to represent Jasper—to prove his innocence.

"Thank you," I say. "And you may call me, simply, Ruby."

It's strange to speak this name, especially to this man who looks at me as if he knows me, as if he senses that behind this name and position is a whole other life, a whole other story.

He smiles another of his enigmatic smiles and bows before exiting the cottage, and I jump up and squeal at the sight of the feast before me. I lose my grip on the sheet, and it falls to the floor as I laugh and shrug. "When in preparation for seducing a priest yet not having to bed a stranger…" I joke to myself, and then I indulge in a chocolate croissant and the most decadent strawberries I've ever tasted—and try to forget the fact that I haven't seen a painting of an angel or what Madam will do if I don't find it.

I fire off a quick text to The Jewel Box messenger service, asking if Madam will allow me to spend more time on the palace grounds to find what I'm looking for. The response is almost immediate.

Enjoy your stay, Evangeline. I expect this means you will have good news for me soon, or else you know what to expect from me.

My palm flies instinctively to the cheek she slapped the first time I questioned her.

"Whatever it takes, Jasper," I say aloud. "I will not lose you, too."

When X extends a hand to help me from the golf cart and into a Rolls-Royce, he raises his brows.

"What?" I ask, skimming the length of my own body, afraid I'd forgotten to dress myself after my feast.

"Nothing, miss. It's just—I'm looking forward to finding you something more befitting a palace guest."

I lower myself into the car as my cheeks flame and my eyes prick with tears. I try to swallow it all back, to not let him see his judgment get to me. But when X situates himself in the driver's seat, the first thing he does is speak to me via an intercom.

"My apologies, miss," he says. "I meant no offense. It is just that if we are to be discreet, it is necessary that you do not stand out in a way that will make the staff ask questions."

I knock on the glass partition that separates us, and he lowers it as he turns to face me. His salt-and-pepper hair lies in neat waves, and that square, rugged jaw is both attractive and reassuring. Somehow I know that whatever happens today, X is on my side. Still, I need to set the record straight.

"I get it," I say. "I'm here to do a job. And I might not be entirely proud of what I need to do to earn a living right now, but I'm not ashamed of the way I look." It's a half-truth. Even if this wasn't always me, I look and feel sexy in these clothes—in the boots. I just wish I was wearing it all for me and not as a means to an end.

His brows draw together, and his jaw tightens. When he looks at me, it is as if he wants to say many things but holds himself back. "If my comment elicited shame, miss, then again, my sincerest apologies. I am your ally. I do hope you see me as such."

I swipe away a tear. "Thank you, X. And can we please cut it with the 'miss'?"

He smiles. "Of course, Ruby. You remind me of Princess Kate."

With that, he turns back to his steering wheel and leads us away from the palace grounds.

Belladonna Square is not unfamiliar to me. I've driven past it. Walked through it. But never have

I stepped foot into one of the shops. It was nothing more than a tourist attraction the few times I'd been in these parts.

"You know," I say as the car rolls to a stop, "even when things were good, they were never great. My father died when Jasper was fifteen and I was only twelve. Jasper grew up and found work doing research at the art museum and I— Well, there aren't many jobs out there for a girl who likes to paint." Especially when her résumé basically reads like a telenovela.

X nods.

"I don't know why I'm telling you this," I add. "I guess I'm just a bit overwhelmed is all."

He exits the vehicle and opens my door, offering a hand as I climb out. Then he holds out a black credit card.

"You're not coming with me?" I ask, eyes wide.

He offers a soft smile and nods toward the closest boutique, a place called Cheri Cheri. "I called ahead and had them put aside all their Monique Mantissa pieces for you. Just go in and tell them who you are, and they will take care of you. This is your day, not mine. Go enjoy."

I can't help but grin, a giddy electricity pumping through my veins. I reach for my bag and realize in all the excitement that I forgot it in the cottage, so I slip the credit card into the cleavage of my bustier.

X chuckles, and I shrug.

"Here goes nothing!" I say and let my confidence buoy me in the direction of the store.

As I enter, my boot heels click on marble floors, and the place smells of jasmine. I close my eyes and inhale, a smile spreading across my face when I'm greeted by a soft, lilting voice.

"May I…help you?"

My eyes open, and there she is, a tall, lithe woman with a chic pixie cut, her ebony hair shining like satin.

"Everything in here is Monique Mantissa," I say, stating the obvious.

She looks me up and down, her painted-on smile morphing into something more like a sneer.

"Are you lost, miss? The Mantissa knockoffs are on Market Street. This is Belladonna Square."

Heat seeps into my veins.

"I know where I am," I insist, trying to still the tremble in my voice. "I'm here to shop." I pull the credit card from my top and brandish it at her. "See?" I say, the volume of my voice escalating. "I have money to spend. On…on Mantissa. On whatever the hell I want."

She backs toward a marble counter, which must be where the transactions take place. "Miss, you have fifteen seconds to leave before I press the security button. After that, you'll have just as long before the Edenvale Police arrive."

My eyes widen. "You're serious. Aren't you?" I ask incredulously.

She snakes behind the counter. "You're down to five seconds, miss." Her eyes narrow. "Four… three…"

I stumble back through the door and bolt to where X dropped me off, pulling at the handle of the door. It's locked. Tears stream down my face as I yank at the door again and again until I feel strong hands grip my shoulders.

I scream as X spins me to face him.

He is my ally. He is my ally. He is my ally.

"I'm done shopping," I gasp between sobs. "I want to go home."

He nods and unlocks the door, helping me inside. When he is back behind the driver's seat, he speaks in a calm, soothing voice.

"When you're ready, Ruby, I want you to tell me what happened."

But I shake my head.

"I will fix this," he adds, and then he picks up a mobile phone. He doesn't close the partition between us, so I hear every word.

"Your Highness, something unexpected has occurred." Pause. "Yes, I did exactly as we'd discussed." Pause. "No, she is too upset to speak. But I know how to make things right. Miss Mantissa owes me a favor. If she is in town, I can have her bring over a collection of samples." Another pause. "Yes, Highness. To the cottage this evening. It shall be done."

The call ends, and X pulls away from Belladonna Square, his eyes focused on the road.

"They treated you poorly in the store, yes?" Rage is clear in his voice.

I sniffle. "Yes."

"You told them I had called ahead, that you were on official palace business?"

"She didn't give me a chance." My tone is biting. "Maybe you didn't mean to shame me, X. But she did. I had money to spend, and her only intention was to make me feel worthless."

His jaw tightens. The muscle flexes at some deep, hidden emotion.

"I am deeply sorry, Ruby. You of all people did not deserve such treatment. I did not think…" He sighs. "Prince Benedict will join you this evening in the cottage for a private shopping spree of sorts."

I force a smile at this while wondering what he means by me of all people.

"It's okay," I say. "If she's not in town or whatever. I have other clothes back at my place…" My voice trails off. Because I was looking forward to this, to being a princess for a day.

But it took only seconds for that woman to remind me that she saw me as nothing more than a whore.

"You deserve better than what happened just now," X says in his mysterious tone.

I used to think that, too, but it's getting harder and harder to believe.

CHAPTER FOUR

Benedict

THE LAST RAYS of the sun blaze across the western horizon as I pad across the palace grounds, ignoring the royal pond with the swan-shaped pleasure boats, the marble fountains filled with ancient Greek and Roman statuary, and the lush hedges clipped into geometric shapes.

Earlier, X filled me in on Ruby's disastrous visit to Belladonna Square, and I'm still pissed. She was judged on an excursion meant to bring her innocent pleasure.

Acid gnaws at my core from my hypocrisy. After all, she's an escort on my payroll, which makes no part of our relationship innocent even if my motives are pure.

The first star appears as I enter the maze. Left. Left. Straight. Right. My footsteps are unerring, the result of a childhood spent chasing Nikolai through these twists and turns, and later both of us running from our youngest brother, Damien, who hurled himself forward, always intent on keeping up, even if it resulted in trip after trip to the infirmary for broken bones.

Damien.

Reckless. Impatient. Unstoppable. A force of nature. Nikolai and I had loved him, perhaps getting him into more trouble than befitting a much younger brother, but always getting him out of it again.

His birth ended our mother's life, yet no one could look upon our youngest brother's face and fail to see the arrogant, brutal features of my father, the king. My Damien may be many things, but no one would ever call *him* a bastard.

Unlike me…

These days, however, we see him only in paparazzi photos. After he bedded our stepsister—also Nikolai's first betrothed—he was banished from Edenvale. His portraits were removed from the halls. The press has a field day with his wild exploits. His fistfights in high-end nightclubs. His drinking binges. His tumultuous romantic affairs. His devotion to fast cars and racing.

My frown deepens as a shadow ahead takes shape, merging into the form of a man.

"Your Highness." X dips his head in his curt version of a bow. No obsequious gestures for him.

"Jesus." I am startled into taking the Lord's name in vain. "Where did you materialize from, thin air?"

A smug smile serves as his response. "Miss Ruby anticipates your arrival. You will find Monique has treated her well. And I will see to it that the saleswoman who mistreated your guest is aware of the commission she lost."

The cobblestone gardener's cottage rises behind

his broad shoulder, a scene from a storybook come to life, a dwelling that would look at home in one of Grimm's very own fairy tales. Every light is ablaze inside the small round windows. My Adam's apple bobs. What will I confront inside? Scraps of lace? Strategically placed silk? Leather?

It takes all my self-control to walk with a steady, measured pace. A young but capable-looking guard stands watch at his post. I recognize him as Gideon from the front gate watchtower, the one with the large strawberry birthmark on one cheek. Good. I'd ordered X to make sure Ruby remains protected during her sojourn, mostly from curious interlopers as our grounds are well fortified. Gideon's inquiring gaze veers in my direction as I rap on the door.

It swings open in an instant. An older woman, raven hair styled in an intricate chignon, sweeps into a curtsy. Monique Mantissa. "Miss Ruby is ready for your inspection." She sidles past me and out into the maze with a throaty giggle. "I believe that you will be most pleased with her selections."

"Allow me to entertain you while the prince makes his examination?" X's voice betrays no hint of innuendo, and yet the fashion designer's breathless sigh is audible as the door snicks shut.

My eyes adjust to the light. The air is rich with perfume: roses, jasmine and lilac penetrate my senses. A floorboard squeaks in the next room. I step forward, steeling myself for sin incarnate.

A fire roars in the hearth, the same color as her shimmering golden silk and lustrous hair. Out of all the possible sights, I never imagined to discover

Ruby dressed in a formal gown, looking every ounce as regal as any queen in Europe.

She truly is a jewel.

Ruby

Heat warms my cheeks as the prince drinks me in with his eyes.

"It's too much," I say. "I told them it was too much. I'm not meant to wear—"

"That gown was made for you and you alone," he says, no hint of irony in his tone. No condescension or judgment. I'm not entirely sure what to do with that.

"Is there no pretense with you, Your Highness?" His dark brows furrow, the reaction endearing. "You say what you mean, mean what you say. You don't let any of the bullshit get in the way." I gasp and cover my mouth. "My apologies, Father."

He smiles and shakes his head. "That won't be necessary. Ruby, this is your home for the next month. I want you to feel safe to be yourself here."

No big deal. Just be myself and find some painting for the Madam. I try to tell myself this isn't a betrayal of my new benefactor but rather a step closer to saving Jasper. It's not as if I'm going to do anything to the portrait. I just have to let the Madam know it's here and where it is. What happens then is beyond me.

I give the prince a once-over—my whole preposterous situation rolling out before me—and then burst out laughing. And there he goes again with the crinkled brow, completely disarming me and making me forget, at least for now, how I ended up here in the first place.

Damn this man for looking so beautiful when he's befuddled.

"It would already be a tall order to ask me to be myself while residing among royalty. But I'm meant to spend the majority of my time here with not only a prince but one who—though not yet a man of the cloth—dresses like he's forever on a pulpit about to give a sermon."

I'm still giggling when he does something so out of character that it stops my laughter and catches my breath all at once.

He smiles.

The whole kingdom—and the entire world for that matter—has been known to swoon for the king's firstborn, Prince Nikolai. They loved him when he was a tabloid playboy, and now that he's proved himself worthy of ruling Edenvale, as well as worthy of his future queen, the public swoons for him even more, myself included. Nikolai Lorentz is a beautiful man who will do great things. But before me stands the man who has always lived in his shadow—who keeps himself there by hiding behind a collar before it is truly his.

And he's the most beautiful man I've ever seen.

"You're wrong, Ruby. This," he says, pointing to the white collar, "is my pretense." He unfastens it and pulls it free.

I smooth out a nonexistent wrinkle in the buttery-soft silk of my gown. "When you take your final vows—" something twists in my gut at the thought "—do you have to wear it all the time?"

Again he grins, though this time the expression is laced with a wistfulness I don't understand.

"No," he says. "Giving my life to the church is my duty. But presiding over the church is also my livelihood. When I'm not performing clerical duties, I'm free to dress as I please." He glances at his attire and then shrugs. "I guess this is easier."

Then he unbuttons his black shirt and removes it. I gasp until I realize that beneath it he wears a white cotton T.

"There," he says, hanging the garment over a high-back leather chair that faces the fire. "No more pretense." He then strolls to a tall oak cabinet against the wall. With wide eyes, I watch the sculpted muscles in his arms flex as he retrieves a decanter of red wine and two crystal goblets. The prince nods toward a small game table, ignoring the clothes strewn about the sofa.

"You can…drink?" I ask, and he laughs, a rich, deep sound that sends an unexpected shiver through me, goose bumps dotting my flesh.

He sets the items on the table and pulls out my chair for me.

"There are many things I can still do once I am a priest," he says. "But, of course—some I cannot."

His eyes darken before they dip to the table as he seats himself across from me. When he looks up again, he forces a smile, but I know the spell is broken, and it's time to get to work. I reach behind and start to lower my zipper.

"Stop," he says. "Not yet."

Because he is my prince and also my employer, I obey.

He pours two goblets of wine and hands one to me.

"Ruby." His voice is gentle. "I'm sorry for what happened in the Square this morning. That was unacceptable."

I press my lips together and shrug. "I didn't belong there," I say matter-of-factly.

He sips his wine and shakes his head. "You belong wherever it is that you want to be."

My throat tightens, and because I don't know how to respond, I take a long, slow swallow of the expensive crimson liquid, as well.

"I hope you did enjoy your private shopping spree of sorts, though."

I grin and stand, offering an exaggerated curtsy in my favorite of all the pieces Monique Mantissa herself gave to me.

"I felt like a princess," I say. "Thank you, Your Highness."

He clears his throat. "Benedict. Please, call me Benedict."

Sure. He's just a guy in my borrowed home, a guy in a great-fitting T-shirt that hugs an always hidden muscular frame, yet he's not hiding it from me. Still, he is more than just Benedict. I can pretend many things, but I cannot ignore his lineage—or my own.

"This gown is beautiful," I tell him. "But for what you've hired me to do, well…" I reach for my zipper again and pull to where it stops just below my hips. I stand, and the dress falls to the floor, revealing what I've been hiding.

No bra. No panties.

"No more pretense," I tell him, and though he stares at me with ravenous eyes, this feels nothing like the ogling, the leering of what I expect from a client. At twenty-two years old, I am not without experience when it comes to men, but that does not mean I ever thought this would be easy. But the prince is nothing like I expected.

I am comfortable—safe beneath his gaze. Whatever happens next, I trust the man before me.

After laying the gown neatly atop the pile of other Mantissa samples, I take my seat across from him, sip from my goblet and note the varying drawers in the small table. I open one up and pull from it a deck of cards. My teeth skim across my bottom lip. Then I smile and raise a brow.

"So, Benedict." I draw out his name, getting a feel for it on my tongue. "Would you like to play a game?"

CHAPTER FIVE

Benedict

RUBY CUTS THE card deck as my features settle into a bemused poker face.

"Truth or dare, my prince?" Her teasing tone intoxicates. Her nipples are the color of raspberries, a ripe red that ignites my appetite.

I've barely taken a sip of the vintage in my hand, yet the room feels like it does a slow spin. I dig my heels into the wool rug and fight back the growing sense of vertigo.

"You know this game?" Her mouth quirks. "Or were you too busy playing polo and competing in fencing tournaments as a child?"

"I preferred the contact sports, boxing and mixed martial arts." I set down my goblet and meet her surprised gaze. "And I choose truth."

Her brows furrow in concentration. "Hmm." She props two cards together, then adds a third and fourth. It takes a moment to realize what she is doing—building a house of cards.

Higher and higher her flimsy walls rise until she pauses, twirling a Queen of Hearts between her fingers. "Have you ever seen a naked woman in the flesh?"

"No." My voice is cool as a glacier. I refuse to play the role of a clumsy, naive schoolboy. This imperious mask is second nature, my default setting since I was a boy. How many years have I worn it? Probably since the time that I informed my private tutor that someday I intended to do great things, lead the Edenvale armies, explore distant jungles, fulfill any number of mad ambitions a young, imaginative boy might nurture.

Except Father had been listening from the doorway to our palace classroom. That night he had me escorted to the monastery that borders our palace ground, and there, in the nave of St. Germain, back-dropped by the mournful sound of Gregorian chants, the head monk informed me that my path in life was chosen. He spoke of the honor I would bring our kingdom by serving as the spiritual advisor to the king himself.

He made it clear in no uncertain terms that this was the role of the second son, and that if I were to stray or reject the family tradition, it would break my father's heart.

Those were the words that he used.

Break. My father's. Heart.

I knew our mother's death during Damien's birth must have cracked that organ into a million pieces. There was no chance that I'd be the one to deliver the death blow.

And so ever since, I've walked the straight and narrow without complaint. I have striven to do what is right, what is expected.

Until now.

"You are serious?" Ruby's eyes widen curiously. "Never?" Her legs part and she runs her fingers up her smooth inner thighs. My heart threatens to break through the bars of my rib cage. "Are you saying that you're an innocent, my sweet prince?"

A pause. "A virgin in the flesh." Not the mind.

Ruby's pussy is bare, utterly devoid of hair—soft, pink and fucking perfect. The second coming could begin outside the windows, and my gaze would stay fixed on her slick skin, the dew sheening the slit between her lips.

"Want to touch?" She flicks the tip of her finger over her mound.

"You know that I cannot." My voice is hoarse.

"But do you want to?" A sliver of curiosity enters her tone, as if she is actually interested in what I want. As if she is doing more than going through the motions of her profession. She is talented, indeed, to make me believe such illusions.

"Yes," I hiss through gritted teeth.

"How?" she pushes. "How would you touch me if you gave in to the temptation?"

I try to maintain my composure with a measured breath, telling myself that voicing what I want is no more than putting words to a thought. It is not the act.

"So light at first," I say, "that you almost wouldn't know I was making contact, like a brushstroke and your body was a canvas. A butterfly wing against summer's first rose."

Her eyes widen, as if I've struck a hidden nerve, but then she relaxes into that coy smile again. "You wouldn't want to claim me?" There is a challenge lurking there. "Graffiti your name? Mark your territory with greedy thrusts?"

I shake my head. "I'd rather bring you pleasure."

She freezes, staring at me as if transfixed. "But why?"

"Because if it is good for you, it would be good for me," I say simply. "My pleasure must hinge on yours." I don't know why, but instinctively I understand that it's the way that I am wired.

A shudder runs through her as she lowers her lashes. "Mmmmm. My prince, you do say all the right things. For a man not experienced in the ways of the flesh, you certainly are getting me all worked up with just your words. Look how wet I am. It feels so good." She rolls her hand with wanton abandon, dips her fingers deeper inside until they circle an engorged, rosy bud. "So wickedly good." She pauses, arching a brow. "Dare me to offer you a taste?" She drags her hand free, shows me her glistening fingers.

Saints take my immortal soul. I burn as if with a fever.

But I sense she is hiding, that she's back to showmanship.

I wonder if she'd enjoy being stripped of her defenses?

I clear my throat. "You take a taste. Describe your flavor."

"Sir?" She pauses, hesitant, a flush heating her own cheeks.

I've caught her off guard. A flare of pleasure rushes through my veins. I get up from the small game table and saunter to the fireplace, resting my elbow on the mantel. "You heard me."

She obeys, and my own pleasure grows sharper than I'd imagined it could.

Ever so slowly, she raises her fingers to her mouth, full lips parting as she sucks on the tips with a deliberate lick.

Hunger flares in me. The tenor of the room shifts. Her coy, artful smile is lost, replaced by a look of shock. Of wonder. Her pupils grow wide, and a flush spreads in the delicate skin between her breasts.

"Describe it."

Her breath hitches at the dominating timbre of my voice. Her gaze turns thoughtful. Inward. And I know she is going to give me the truth.

"Sweet," she begins slowly, "almost like wildflower honey." Her voice is a shy whisper. "But slightly spicy with a salty tang."

My tongue presses against my teeth. It's absurd how natural this feels—me, fully clothed and standing, towering over a naked woman pleasuring herself at my command. It's like opening up a door and walking into a part of myself that's always been here, waiting for me to find the way. "Keep going," I grind out. "Tell me your darkest fantasy."

"You've already had a turn," she says with a fake pout. "I did the dare." Her hands are already sliding back as if of their own accord, spreading her most secret part, revealing every inch of the tantalizing landscape to my view. She is so wet I can hear it, the sucking slide of her fingers. Perhaps she has done this five hundred times to five hundred different men, but tonight, in this moment, she is mine.

And if her soaking wet pussy is any indication, she loves every second.

The fire beats against my legs but is a cool breeze compared to the blaze in my cock.

"This is my game now, angel. My rules." My voice is kind but inflexible. The log in the hearth hisses and pops, but hellfire doesn't scare me, not now when salvation lies between Ruby's parted legs. "I want you to expose not only your body to me, but also your mind."

Her thick lashes flutter. "You do?"

I incline my head. "I have a theory that you might be as desirable on the inside as on the outside. So tell me…" I lower my voice an octave. "What fantasy makes your thighs quiver, your nipples tighten into tight, aching peaks? Let me inside. Let me see."

"What?" Her voice quavers, her toes curl against the thick wool rug. "What do you want to see?"

I cross the small room as if in a dream. Then I'm standing above her, my hand tilting her chin, ensuring her gaze is fixed on me and me alone. "A glimpse of your soul."

Ruby

He holds a hand out to me, and I take it, letting him guide me from the chair, out of the hearth room—and to my bed. With a look, he tells me to lie on the plush duvet as he moves toward the rocking chair under the window.

"Relax," he says softly. "Close your eyes and let me inside you the only way I am permitted to do so. Show me what you'd want me to give you if only I could."

I swallow hard and nod, my chest tightening at

the unexpected emotions brewing within me—my core burning with unbridled need.

This is not what I expected. Everything up until now has been a show. But what he's asking…

"Touch yourself, angel. Touch and tell me what it is you desire."

I think of his words, that his touch would be like brushstrokes on a canvas. He couldn't have known. Could he? That painting is my passion, but this—using my body for money—is the only way to save my family.

My lips part as my finger circles them softly. "I want featherlight kisses to start. Ones that tell me with each sweep of his mouth on mine that I am what matters. That for all I do to protect those I love, there is someone out there whose one true desire is to protect me. To love me."

The truth falls from my lips without pretense, and I don't know where it is coming from. I've never said any such thing aloud…to anyone.

"Continue," Benedict says, breaking the silence.

So I do.

"His kisses trail down my neck to my breasts." I give one of my nipples a soft pinch and gasp. "He takes me into his mouth, his teeth nipping, tongue swirling." I lick my thumb and forefinger, rolling them around the peaked nipple of my other breast, pinching harder this time. My pelvis bucks upward, and I moan. "More," I say. "I tell him I need more, that the teasing is driving me mad, and the kisses continue, lower and lower. They are still soft, still sweet, and though he hungers for me, he is in control. And he will tease because as much as I beg, he knows I love every second of it."

I've never let my imagination run away like this. Fantasies aren't anything I have the luxury to think about, let alone voice.

My thumb presses my swollen clit, still teasing just as I wish he would—as I wish Benedict could—and I writhe.

"More," I whimper. "Oh God, more. Benedict, I need more!"

I gasp but keep my eyes squeezed shut. Because in my mind—in this never-before-realized dream—it is he who kneels over me. It is his hand between my legs, his fingers aching to pump inside me. It's this stranger who allowed me to sleep like a queen last night and dress like a princess today.

Prince Benedict wants to know my soul.

I know better than to think this fantasy could ever be realized by a celibate prince, by a man who does not get to touch, let alone love.

But for tonight I can pretend.

"Please. Benedict." I say his name again, using the cloak of darkness behind closed lids as my safety.

"Take control, angel," he says, his deep, velvety voice carrying an unmistakable ache. "Show me what you want me to do."

I suck two fingers down to the knuckle and then plunge them, wet, between my legs, sinking deep into my warmth.

I cry out.

The show is over. This is so real I can feel it in every nerve, every pulse of blood through my veins. So I do the unthinkable and open my eyes, propping myself up on my free elbow, so my stare locks with his.

His eyes burn into mine, veritable flames igniting something in me that refuses to be extinguished. As my fingers pump harder, his hands grip the armrests of the chair, knuckles white and nails digging into the wood.

"This is what I'd have you do. With your hands. Your mouth. Your cock." I slide my fingers out, drenched in my own arousal, and swirl them fiercely around my clit. My head falls back, and the arm that supports my weight begins to shake. "I can't—" I say. "I can't last much longer. Make me come," I plead. "Make me fucking come, Benedict!" My voice is not my own. It is something savage, a need I didn't know existed until now.

"I cannot," he says, but the words are a primal growl.

"Do it!" I command, my eyes on his again. "With your words, Benedict. Just your words. Tell me what you would do to finish me off. They are nothing more than innocent words."

He leans forward, hands still glued to the armrests, and I can see that his pupils have grown so large his eyes look black. "Fuck." He grits his teeth. "Fuck."

But he says nothing more. So I collapse on the bed, one hand spreading myself open for him to see, the other sending me over the edge and into oblivion.

I don't hold back. I don't stifle my scream as I fill myself with one finger, then two, then three until I buck against my palm.

When I finally slide my hand free with a shudder,

I lie there, limp and languid from the most perplexing orgasm I've ever experienced.

What does it mean that I enjoyed what just happened…or that I wanted it to be his hands on me instead of my own? I was prepared to give him a good show, but instead, despite the undeniable pleasure of the evening, I'm left wanting more.

"That was…different," I say, my voice back to its soft lilt. "I've never done anything like that before. I assure you." I laugh, my eyes still shut, lids heavy as the aftermath threatens to carry me off to sleep before he can respond.

I open my eyes to gauge the prince's reaction, to congratulate him on his restraint.

But the chair is empty. And when I hear the front door slam, I wonder if the first night of our arrangement will be the last.

Because Benedict is gone.

CHAPTER SIX

Benedict

I KNEEL IN front of the high altar of the royal chapel. The tabernacle is open, exposing the Eucharist, the consecrated bread transmogrified into the body of Christ. I need him to see what I have done this night, reveled in lust, taken pleasure in bending a woman to my will, woken my dormant craving for sexual domination. As Ruby undulated in her sheets, her pale skin flush with the intensity of her orgasm, a single refrain played through my mind.

What would her wet pussy feel like throbbing around my own fingers?

Would she enjoy it as much as what she'd just done to herself? Would I?

"No!" I don't realize that I've spoken out loud until the word echoes through the marble-walled nave. Even now, even here, my thoughts are polluted. I cover my hands over my face. How can I be what my duty demands? Why can't I conquer these urges?

If I stray from my path, where will it lead?

A frustrated moan escapes my gritted teeth. I am so fucking weak.

"Can I be of assistance?"

I'm on my feet before my next breath, hands braced against the altar rails. "Who said that?" The voice comes from near the pulpit. Could it be the miracle I'm looking for, the gift of salvation? "Lord? Is that you?"

The low, deep chuckle is familiar. X steps from the shadows. "Careful, Highness," he says with a wry smile. "You want to give me a God complex?"

"Where'd you come from?" I snap, embarrassed at my error.

"Couldn't sleep, and you were otherwise…occupied." He shrugs. "So I took a stroll through the catacombs."

I blink. "Where?"

He saunters down the altar steps and sits in the first pew, crossing a foot over his knee. As always, he is dressed in an impeccable suit. It would be tempting to dismiss him as continuing to have fun at my expense, but the dust coating his hair makes his salt-and-pepper locks appear saltier than normal.

"The ancient catacombs beneath the chapel. As far as I can tell, they've been sealed up since the early seventeenth century by your nine-times great-grandfather King Ivor the Protector."

I cross my arms. "I haven't been down there. We were thought too young to attend my mother's funeral."

He gives me a look of sympathy. "Many of the tunnels are in disrepair, and I encountered a rat the size of a cocker spaniel. That's when I exited through a secret passage here beneath the high altar beside the statue of Saint Everly, the patroness of our realm."

X has been a fixture of the castle since I was a teenager. And yet he is an utter mystery to me. "What were you doing there if it is so dangerous?"

"The more interesting question is whether you are enjoying the company of Miss Ruby. You might not be aware that she comes from The Jewel Box, a Rosegate pleasure house valued for its discretion but also quality. All the girls there go by the names of precious stones." He gives his chin a musing rub. "I've had the good fortune to while away many a pleasant afternoon with a most diverting escort named Pearl. She used to insist on wearing nipple clamps and would do anything to get a chance to go under my flogger."

I am ashamed to realize that I know little about Miss Ruby. I can describe every inch of her perfect body, but I haven't the first clue about her actual life. I clear my throat, deciding to hide my discomfiture behind a question. "You consort with escorts regularly?"

My bodyguard is an enigma. I knew my brother was a favorite of the ladies, but apparently, when it came to his most trusted bodyguard, the apple didn't fall far from the tree.

Not for the first time, I wonder why he requested a transfer to my security detail.

X's laughter is amused, not unkind. "I consort with women regularly. Some of them are escorts. Some are not. All of them are quite skilled at…consorting."

I stare blankly for a few seconds, struggling to process his words. Again, I can't help but wonder, Who is this guy? Like Ruby, I have never wondered much about X's past. He was my brother's bodyguard, but it seems there is more than meets the eye. The tabernacle bores into my spine, the eyes of the Lord waiting to judge my next move. I have questions that require answers, but I can't ask them in here.

"We will continue this conversation out of the church."

I stride toward the thick carved doors as X replies, "Very good, sir."

Outside, the night air is crisp. The wind blowing over the surrounding snowcapped peaks cool my heated face, but I won't lie to myself. My shiver has nothing to do with the temperature.

"You do not tie yourself to one woman?" I know not everyone believes in monogamy. My elder brother, Nikolai, certainly didn't...until he met his Kate that is.

X adjusts his tie, his expression blank. "I am not opposed to...tying," he says, the corner of his mouth quirked into a knowing grin. "But I'm normally the one who makes the knots."

Envy hits me with blunt force. "The stories you could tell," I mutter, but my tone does not escape him.

"I know you are well-read, but there is something to be said for experience, for true knowledge. You aren't a priest yet, Your Highness."

Though X is overstepping, I do not call him on it. Instead, I swallow hard at the idea. I have so many questions. They press against my skull, threatening to crack the bone.

I want to know more, but I need to resist.

"The choice of celibacy is not one to take lightly,"

X says, his voice firm. "You can yield to her. There is no harm in seeing what you'd be missing."

But I can't afford to give in to the bonfire of my sexual urges. If I do, I might burn down my carefully scripted future. Instead, I turn wordlessly and escape back to my tower that tonight feels more like a prison than ever before.

Ruby

The drowsy aftermath of my orgasm is replaced by something unsettling, something that not only keeps me from sleep but drives me from the cottage altogether. The summer night is cool, but my body is still alight from the mere thought of Benedict's touch, so I wear nothing but a long silk dressing gown, another gift from Monique Mantissa.

Thanks to X's coaching this afternoon, I've learned my way out of the maze—well, with only having to backtrack twice. I'd say that's pretty impressive for my first day. Though the sun has long set, the brilliant moon lights the palace grounds in a soft glow. I make my way to the gardens behind the palace itself, not sure what I'm hoping to find. Benedict on an evening stroll, trying to clear his thoughts just as I am? But all is quiet but for the guards on patrol. I stare up at the tower where I know the prince resides, and for a second I consider climbing that spiral staircase and knocking on his door.

For what? He does not want to see you. That is why he left.

Yet I cannot deny that I wish to see him.

Instead, I decide to give him space. Back at the

cottage, I can call Camille to check in, see if we have any new leads on Jasper's case. This, I remind myself, is why I am here. For my family.

So I make a hasty retreat. Once there, it takes me only one try to get through the maze and to the cottage. I only now realize there is no guard on patrol at this hour, and once I'm inside, that unsettling chill returns. Though this time it is different.

Something is different. I can feel it. And it is in my room where I find it.

I flip on the light, the space brighter than it was before, and then realize Benedict and I were lit only by the moon. The rocking chair, the one from which he watched me—was it not closer to the window before? Benedict himself had leaned forward for a better view, but had he actually moved the chair?

I circle the benign piece of furniture, sure that there was no room to step behind it before, and a floorboard creaks, a sound I should have heard had Benedict rocked against it.

I bend to examine it, and the wooden slat comes up easily in my hand.

I scramble backward, gasping at what cannot be real, but I peek over into the open space again and see not the foundation of an architectural structure but what looks like a cavernous hole with no end.

Then, as if from the bowels of hell, comes the terrifying yet distant sound of a woman's triumphant laughter.

Without another thought, I am running—out the door, through the maze and straight to where I swore I would not go. I don't even remember climbing the stairs when I'm already pounding on his door. Maybe

I hallucinated it. Maybe the sound was just the wind. But my skin is covered in goose bumps and my heart is threatening to crack my sternum.

"Benedict!" I cry, no time for propriety. "Benedict, please. Open the door!"

In seconds he is there, bare but for cotton pajama pants, his chest beaded with sweat, but I'm too frightened to react to his body the way I know I would have only a short time ago.

"Ruby," he says, his eyes widening. "What is it?"

I hug my torso, shivering now—from the chill in the air? Fear? I'm not even sure.

"Did you go to the cottage?" I ask, hoping for logic to rearrange my frantic thoughts. "Did you go to my room?"

His brows furrow, and he shakes his head.

"I— After you left, I went for a walk. And…" I take a shuddering breath. After what my life has become these past two months, I'm starting to trust that things will only get worse. "I think someone broke in while I was gone."

A muscle in his jaw ticks. He looks over his shoulder and then at me.

"Come in," he says. "You are safe here." He steps aside and closes the door. "Follow me."

He moves in front of me, and I gasp as he leads me from the entryway, as my eyes rest on the raised welts that cover his back.

He says nothing until we are in a modest bedchamber. The walls are bare but for a crucifix on the wall by a lone window. The bed is large but without any trappings of royalty. Just plain white sheets and a quilt. He sits me on the edge of the bed and moves a good distance from me, crossing his arms.

"Tell me what happened," he says, not bothering to acknowledge the new elephant in the room.

"Tell me what happened to you," I say.

He sighs. "Nothing," he says softly. "Nothing more than purging myself of my guilt."

My hand flies to my mouth as I stifle another gasp.

"My tormented soul isn't your concern, Ruby. I hired you to do a job, and you performed as expected. Now tell me what you are doing here."

His words bite, though I know they shouldn't. They are nothing more than the truth.

"When I got home," I tell him, "something felt wrong. And when I went to my room, the chair— your chair—was not where you'd left it. At least, I don't think it was." As I speak, I realize I sound less convincing by the second. But then I remember the floorboard. "There was a squeaky piece of wood in the floor behind the chair, and I thought it odd that it hadn't sounded when you were there, because I swear your chair was right over it, so I pulled it up and—"

"Let me guess. And you found the catacombs?" He raises a brow and grins.

I stand up in a huff. "I just ran here frightened for my life, and you're joking around?" I ask. The idea of laughter seems too ridiculous to mention. It must have been the wind and my own overactive imagination.

I turn to storm out, realizing I won't find comfort here, but Benedict grabs my wrist.

"Wait," he says.

I face him but say nothing more.

"There is a chance I may have moved my chair closer to you." His expression darkens. "I don't remember. You bewitched me with that show you put on—inserting me into your fantasy. I probably couldn't have told you what day it was while I was in that room, let alone whether or not I moved a chair."

"But the catacombs? That dark hole under the floor?"

He nods, a soft smile taking over his features. "There is not only a maze above the ground but one beneath it, as well. They run from under the palace to the far reaches of the grounds. I assure you that is all you saw beneath the cottage, and I can almost assure you it was I who moved the chair."

I sigh, and he finally drops my wrist. "I guess that all makes sense." And it does, though I'm still uneasy. "I guess...I'll head back and go to sleep."

He reaches for my cheek but stops short.

"You are still frightened."

I nod.

"Then you will sleep here." He gestures toward the bed. "I was going to sleep on the floor anyway," he adds.

At this, I want to reach for him, to ask him to forgive himself for nothing more than wanting what he cannot have. But I know that will only cause him further distress. And because I do not want to be alone in what now feels like too strange of a place, I agree.

"I do have one condition," I say, and he bows his head slowly. "You need to let me tend to your wounds. There are so many bruises." For a moment I wonder if this is the hardest he's punished himself yet. "I don't want you marred on my account." He opens his mouth to protest, but I shake my head. "Let me—let me do something good," I say.

His shoulders relax, and he points toward the direction from where we came. "The bathing room is on the left. You will find supplies in there, healing salves and such."

I smile and turn toward the door, and that's when I see what's on the wall…what wasn't in my line of sight when we entered the room.

This is what I was sent to find, but now that I see it, I realize that whatever the story is behind the painting, it's more than I anticipated.

It is not only the image of an angel…but it is one who wears my face.

CHAPTER SEVEN

Benedict

THERE IS A loud thump as my bedroom door slams shut. I whirl around to find Ruby crumpled against it, hands pressed to her face, her cheeks drained of all color.

"What is it?" I demand. My heart is in my throat. She seemed fine a moment ago, composed even.

"The portrait…" She keels forward as if to swoon. "You own one of Vernazza's Guardian Angels paintings?"

I blink slowly, unable to comprehend the depth of emotion in her voice. "You're a fan of Giuseppe Vernazza's work?" Vernazza was regarded as the great artist of our age until his unfortunate death a decade ago, losing control of his car and wrapping it around a tree along the Nightgardin border. A waste to lose such a gifted prodigy before his time.

Her laugh is without humor and goes on and on, the hysterical edge slashing my peace of mind. "You could say that," she gasps. "Vernazza was my father. Look closer at the painting. Tell me, does it remind you of anyone?"

I transfer my gaze from her beautiful face to that of the angel, the one that has so often served as both my temptation and my salvation—and my heart gives a dull thud. What a fool I have been not to see what was right under my nose. Ruby's face…the angel's face, good God, they are one and the same. No wonder she appeared so familiar the moment she removed the wig. My insides churn.

"He painted my features as he imagined they would one day look. His imagination came close to the truth, right?"

It's as if my world has flipped its axis and down is up and up is down. "I didn't know."

How could I have been so blind?

"Of course not." She winds her arms around her legs, hugs her knees to her chest. "Who would imagine the daughter of Europe's most famous painter since Pablo Picasso would make a living by selling her body?"

"Why do *you* work for The Jewel Box?"

Her eyes darken. "My father died."

"Rest his soul." I make the sign of the cross. "A terrible accident. I shall pray for him."

"Accident?" She pushes herself to standing, her features fierce, shining with hidden fire. "My father drove that same route between Nightgardin and Rosegate at least once a week to deal with patrons. He took expert care of that car. No. That wasn't a mere accident that claimed his life. The weather was calm. The sun shining. He was murdered. Someone tampered with his brakes!"

My shoulder blades slam together. "You have proof?"

A sob escapes her. "Only the truth in my heart. There is no proof. No motive. Mother died not long after my birth, and all I had after Father was my brother. J-J-J-Jasper." As the name leaves her tongue, her weeping grows.

"Jasper Vernazza." I frown. "This name, it's familiar to me."

"His fate wasn't as dramatic as Father's. He still lives, if you can call being locked in a cage like an animal a life. He was a minor news story this past year until we lost his case and they locked him up. He was an art historian caught stealing a painting from my father's collection in the Musée des Beaux-Arts. They say he wanted to sell it to a black market dealer in Hong Kong, but my brother reveres museums and Father's legacy. It doesn't make sense." She wipes her eyes. "The portrait he was accused of stealing was another angel, actually. My father painted a whole series of them."

"And each one is superb. I've studied his works." I've seen most of them over the years. They are all of Ruby's dreamy, heavenly face contrasted with a different hyperrealistic dystopian cityscape.

"My brother was set up, I just don't know why." With one shuddering inhalation she composes herself. "Anyway, this is not your concern. I remember your library. Art is not the only thing you study. You are fascinated by tales of pleasure, as well. I swear on my life you know more about the erotic arts than Madam herself."

I nod. "I seek to understand beauty, for to know beauty is to know the face of God." Strange. Until this moment I've never articulated this idea, either in thoughts or words.

She ducks her chin, a little shy, and stares up between her curtain of golden hair. "And to you, pleasure is beautiful?"

"I believe there is a sacred union of the body and soul when it comes to sex." I begin to pace, assuming the tone of the professor, not a stretch considering I hold a PhD in Sacred Theology from the University of Edenvale. "Sexuality has the power to be as explosive as dynamite, and when used properly, it can be a tool that moves mountains. And if used improperly, it can grow volatile and wreak untold destruction."

Her brows knit. "Yet you deny yourself."

"I have what you could call an arranged marriage," I say wryly. "My intended bride is to be the church."

She lets out a frustrated huff, opening the door and disappearing for a moment. There is a rustling from the bathroom, and she emerges clutching a small vial. "I found arnica." She uncorks the lid and takes a tentative sniff. "It appears to be mixed with lavender oil."

"A medicinal ointment." I nod my head. "Useful to treat all manner of aches and pains."

"Let me do this." She clutches the bottle, eyes wide. "Heal you."

I take a step backward and find myself in a corner. "Why do you want to?"

"Because I think you are a good man. And the marks on your back make me want to cry. They also make me angry at God because why would He demand you to punish yourself for feelings that you admit are natural?"

"Sacrifice is holy," I tell her, repeating the lessons I've been taught my whole life.

"If lust is an impulse that must be literally beaten from your flesh, then you are giving God something that is unclean, unholy. Why would He want such an offering?"

I bite the inside of my cheek, impressed at the depth of her impassioned response. "You'd make quite the scholar, Miss Vernazza."

"Don't call me that," she snaps. "Not anymore. Now I am simply Ruby." She strides forward, pouring ointment into her open palm. "And you are trying to distract me from my task like a naughty patient. Sit." Her tone brokers no dissent.

I move to a wooden chair and sink to the seat.

"Let's see how extensive the damage is." She peruses my back, her long hair tickling my bare skin. Her silence stretches for the length of a minute. "Benedict," she says, my name a sigh from her lips. "So much pain." Her fingertips press on my throbbing skin, the welts from the whip. The lavender scent of the ointment floods my senses, but is nothing compared to the intense vibrations sent out across my flesh from her soft, circular massage.

"Let's see if we can make you feel better," she whispers in my ear.

Ruby

His skin is like fire under my touch, the raised welts tearing at my heart as my fingers travel over each one.

"Benedict," I say, but I don't know what comes next. His name falls so easily from my lips, yet I know the skin I touch blazes not only with the heat of desire but that of intense, overwhelming guilt. It is the skin not just of a man but of royalty; a world in which I do not belong, save for my likeness hanging on his wall.

His head droops.

"Have I hurt you?" I ask, afraid I am doing more harm than good.

He gives his head a soft shake. "The way you say my name," he says.

"I'm sorry," I blurt. "I meant Your Highness."

"No," he assures me. "It is not that." I listen and continue to massage the salve over his wounds. "The way you say Benedict, it makes me feel…known."

"Oh," I say, my hands pausing but never leaving his skin. "I'm not sure what to do with that," I admit.

"Nothing." He lets out a bitter laugh. "Only God can truly know me," he says. "That is my chosen path."

I step around the chair to face him, and he lifts his head.

"Did you really choose that path, Benedict? Or was it chosen for you?"

His green eyes are a storm of emotion, yet his words are the picture of calm.

"How I got here is of no matter," he says. "This is my path, and I shall not stray."

I kneel and place my hands on his thighs. He takes a ragged breath, and I expect him to push me away. But he doesn't. So I decide to push. Not because of what the Madam assigned me to do and not to push Benedict toward failure if, in fact, this is not what he wants. The entire realm envies the royal family, yet I wonder what anyone in a position such as Benedict—or any member of his family for that matter—gets to choose.

"If you had a choice right now," I ask, "if you could have something you wanted that you thought you didn't deserve, what would it be?"

He leans against the chair and winces. He is in more pain than he's letting on.

"Is this more truth or dare?" he asks, forcing himself to smile through the pain, but his feigned attempt at levity does not work on me.

"No games," I say. "We already did that, so I'm technically off the clock. I want you to choose something for you."

He places his hands atop mine, his fingers circling my wrists.

"To voice such a thing would be selfish."

I laugh even as tears prick at my eyes. How many times have I wanted something just for myself only to give it up for someone else? To have the luxury of acting on one selfish wish? I would take it in an instant.

"Then be selfish, Benedict. You are not a priest, not yet. And from what I know of your religion, until you take your final vows, you may do as you please. This is a new millennium. You're young, fairly easy on the eyes." I grin. "You could have any woman you want, and yet you deny yourself. Why?"

He grips me tighter, lifting my palms from his legs.

"To save myself for God," he says through gritted teeth.

"No." I shake my head. "I don't believe that. After what you had me do tonight, I know you want. I know you are tempted. Why not act on those temptations while you can?"

Now he does throw my hands from him, and he springs from the chair, pacing the length of the room. He runs a hand through his hair, tearing at it as he does.

"Benedict," I say, standing and heading toward the wall. "Benedict, you're scaring me."

He stops before me, chest heaving and his emerald eyes wide.

I squeeze my eyes shut and try to burrow into the wall to escape whatever is coming. I have forgotten myself tonight—forgotten who I am and what it is that I do. I have forgotten that this man, this prince, is nothing more than my client, and a displeased client takes his frustrations out on the whore. I have heard the stories. I have seen the aftermath. It's more than a surprising slap across the face from the Madam.

I just didn't think it would happen to me so soon.

"Ruby," he says, his voice as gentle as a whisper, and I open my eyes. My hands are still balled into fists, and I realize I'm holding my breath. "Heavens, Ruby, no. Did you think— I could never—"

A tear escapes the corner of my eye, my fear finally getting the best of me, and he swipes it away with a thumb. Only then do I exhale.

"Madam leaves punishment up to the client. If he is not satisfied…"

But I also factor in her own dissatisfaction—what she will do if I don't let her know about the painting now that I know where it is.

He brushes my hair from my face, each stroke of his hand telling me that he is different. That I am safe.

"I am not a client," he says. "Not for the rest of this evening."

I exhale. "But you were so angry. And it happened so quickly, I thought… I mean, I was getting myself ready for the worst."

He raises his head to the ceiling—or, most likely, the heavens—and whispers Latin words I do not understand. Then his eyes find mine again. The storm is gone. He is once again the picture of calm.

"There are two reasons why I deny myself the pleasures of the flesh though I've not yet taken my vows. I would like to tell them to you."

He is so close, his woodsy, earthy scent intoxicating me. If he is not a client right now, then what is he? Why is it that in his presence, I long for him to know me, as well?

I nod.

"First," he says, and his hand skims the silk sleeve of my robe until he finds my clenched fist. I relax and let him take my hand in his. "To maintain my virtue until my vows—it is the ultimate test of strength and will. I want to be strong enough for this. I want to give myself to the Lord wholly and completely, which means I will not give myself to another."

"Okay," I say softly, accepting that this is a choice he gets to make, and if anyone can understand that, I can.

"The second reason," he says, his head dipping toward mine, "is that I am terrified to know what I am missing."

"Oh," I say, eyes wide.

"I will not give you my virtue," he says.

"I know."

"But for just a moment, I do want to be selfish."

"What do you want, Benedict?" His nearness is almost too much to bear.

"A kiss," he says.

I know without asking that I will be his first, and I know the slippery slope down which this could lead.

But I want to be selfish, too, just for a moment.

"Take what you want," I tell him.

"First tell me your name. Your real name."

And because I want to be known, too, if only for tonight, I say it.

"Evangeline."

"A beautiful name." He grins. "My angel, Evangeline." And with that, his fingers circle my wrists again, sliding my arms up the wall so he holds my hands over my head. I am captive to my prince, and yet I've never felt more free.

My nipples harden beneath my silk dressing gown, and I cannot ignore the throb between my legs.

His head dips farther until I can feel his warm breath against my skin, and when his lips brush hesitantly against mine, I thank whatever God there is that Benedict is holding me in place, because my knees give out. I whimper, and my prince takes what he needs.

CHAPTER EIGHT

Benedict

I PRESS MY forehead to hers. Evangeline Vernazza. I kiss her again, deeper this time and more urgent. She responds with a hunger not unlike my own, her sweet tongue flicking and caressing mine until I groan. My hands leave hers to tangle in her silky hair. Our breath mingles, feverishly hot.

At last I give in and allow myself to cup one of her perfect breasts, soft as rose petals, and her body bows. So responsive. So passionate. I growl my approval, unable to get enough.

I'll never get enough.

How many times have I flicked through dusty leather-bound books of poetry, scoffing at the over-inflated metaphors and purple prose? Now…now I finally understand those poor poets, and pity everyone who attempted to capture this feeling of two souls merging with mere words.

I dip to kiss her arched neck, trace my tongue along her pulse. Every inch of me burns, but this does not feel like hell.

No.

This is a heaven I never could have imagined.

Even though my control hangs by the barest thread, I refuse to let it snap. Tonight I have glimpsed what can exist between a man and a woman.

This moment must be enough.

As much as I want to forget the world and burn in her arms, I am bound to my duty, my destiny as the second son to Edenvale's king.

Ruby…no—Evangeline…my sweet angel and unexpected jewel, opens her eyes.

"Why did you stop?" she whispers, brows knitting.

Because if I didn't, I'd be inside you to the hilt. I would throw away my entire future.

But I don't say that. Instead, my features settle into a familiar mask. I might not look much like my youngest brother, but suddenly I understand the hard smile, the shuttered eyes that Damien used. My gut twists in understanding. My little brother hid the secrets of his heart just like I hide my own now, for I am falling for a woman whom I pay to tempt me. Common sense would say this feeling is nothing but lust.

But fuck common sense.

There is more to heaven and earth than what meets the eye, and the saints, I am sure, are laughing their holy asses off.

My lips twist into a bitter smile. Of course I'd imagine myself falling head over heels after a mere two days. If she touches my cock, I might propose marriage.

"Go to bed," I bark, ignoring her questioning

gaze. It's not fair. But it is my right. I am Prince of Edenvale. My word is law here.

She senses the authority in my voice and dips her head. "As you wish, Highness…but…" She dares to glance between her thick fringe of lashes, a glitter of mischief, as if she's not as subservient as her posture might pretend. "Don't you want to join me?"

She'll be the death of me.

"I will check on you later. For now, get some sleep Find some peace. One of us deserves that much."

Before she can ask another question, I turn on my heel and stalk from the room.

When I enter the library, I'm surprised to find the antique lamps are lit. X glances from his perch in a leather chair. He assumes a more casual pose than I am used to seeing, one of his legs slung over the chair's arm, and for once in his life, he looks startled.

"Benedict!" He bounds to his feet and clicks his heels. "Did I or did I not see Miss Ruby enter your bedchamber?"

I incline my head. "She is in my bed this very moment."

"And yet, you are here?" He does not ask the question he wants answered most, yet I know it hangs between us. "Have you gone mad?"

Perhaps I have.

I relax my shoulders, grateful for an opportunity to unburden my chaotic mind. "I needed space from temptation."

"Forgive me." His mouth purses. "But is that not the whole point of having her around?"

"I don't know!" I snarl through gritted teeth, then whirl and punch the wall. "I know nothing." The pain steadies me, so I do it again, three times in quick succession.

"Feel better?" X asks, the corner of his mouth curling up in amusement.

"No." I open and shut my hand a few times. "What are you doing here, anyway?"

He smiles lazily, but I swear I sense a troubled soul lurking behind his hooded eyes. "I am your personal bodyguard. And tonight I decided to do a little light reading while you were otherwise…ahem… occupied."

I cross the room and swipe the book from his chest. *"The Asca Mountains: A History.* What's this about? Do you plan to do an overland hike into Nightgardin?" The Asca Mountains provide the ancient border surrounding our old enemy to the north. In fact, the forbidding peaks have long kept Edenvale safe from the various feuds across Europe. Back when the great Carthaginian General Hannibal crossed the Alps during the Second Punic War, he ransacked the Romans because he wasn't able to breach the perilous Ascas.

"One can never know too much about local geography," X says enigmatically. "How about you? What brings you here when you have a willing woman warming your bed? Back before he met Princess Kate, your brother Nikolai would have disappeared for a week if he had struck upon such good fortune."

I set my jaw. "I am not my brother."

"No, you aren't." X appraises me with a shrewd eye. "You have too much of your mother in you."

My throat constricts. Perhaps if she'd lived, none of what has occurred in my family would have ever happened. Damien wouldn't have grown reckless and self-destructive from carrying the crushing burden of guilt for her death. Nikolai would have been saved earlier from his wanton bad-boy behavior. Perhaps she'd have even softened Father to my existence, encouraged me to walk a different life path despite my duty to serve the church.

But daydreaming about what-ifs is a luxury not afforded a member of the royal family. "You knew my mother?" I ask.

"She was a wonderful and kindhearted woman who loved her children more than life itself."

"How about my father?" I don't know where this rush of anger comes from, but it hits me with a tidal-wave force. "Tell me. Did you happen to be acquainted with the Captain of the Guard?"

X rises to his feet, the ancient book clattering from his lap. "Is that truly what you think of your mother? That she was unfaithful to her husband and king?"

Shame circulates in my veins.

"It's what everyone whispers," I challenge. "They say that my mother played the whore while my father the king was away on diplomatic duty. That I am the living, breathing testament to her transgression. Isn't that why my cuckolded father insists that I walk this lonely path, destined never to love or be loved, only to atone for the sins of a woman that I barely remember and a man that I have never met? My duty is atonement."

There it is, the bitter truth, out at last.

"Benedict..." X winces. "Is this what you truly believe?"

"It is what I know," I say with quiet resignation. "It is my life and has been since I was old enough to understand the burden I bear."

He looks as if he means to say more, but as he opens his mouth, a muffled but bloodcurdling scream pierces through the ceiling.

Ruby. Evangeline.

We race to the stairs and fly to my bedchamber.

Evangeline

I don't recognize the room or the bed, not even the thin silk gown that covers my otherwise naked form. But she stares at me from where I clutch the pillow to my body. The angel stares, and I can do nothing but scream.

"Ruby!" a rough voice cries, but I do not know this name. I do not know the man who speaks it. "Go to her, Benedict. I will search for intruders."

A strong hand grips my shoulder, and I thrash against it, crying out until my throat is raw.

"Evangeline!" He is stronger than I am, pulling me to him even as I let go of the pillow and beat against his chest. "Evangeline!" he cries again, and something deep within awakens as recognition blooms, as the warmth of his touch breaks through the icy fear.

I stop fighting, and my shoulders droop as I sink into him, my arms wrapping tight around his neck.

"Benedict," I say, trembling, my senses returning.

"Shh, angel. You're safe now." He strokes my hair and cradles me in his arms as I try to catch my breath, the screams and sobs finally subsiding. "X," he says over my shoulder. "A glass of water, please."

"Yes, Highness," I hear, now recognizing the other male voice as that of Benedict's bodyguard. "All windows are secure, as is the door. I suspect it was only a dream."

Seconds later X returns, handing Benedict the water, which he gingerly brings to my lips.

"Drink," he says, and I do. My throat burns and my vision is still blurry from the tears, but I know where I am now, that I am safe, if only for the moment.

But the angel in the painting is still here—staring, judging. She knows I will betray my prince. And dream or no dream, I know I'm right. It's all too coincidental—what has happened to my family and now this portrait the Madam wants, a portrait so clearly of me.

"They will come for me," I say softly after a few sips. "They came for my father, my brother. Soon I will be next."

Benedict sets the water on the night table next to the bed, and I cling to him even tighter.

"This is not the first time you've had such a dream," he says, a statement rather than a question.

I shake my head. "It has been some time, though. I thought I'd rid myself of the nightmares years ago after Jasper found a wonderful doctor who helped me find peace with my father's death. He is a good big brother, you know. He's taken care of me since I was a young teen."

I bury my head in Benedict's chest, taking in his soothing woodsy scent, cedar and fresh-cut pine.

"His imprisonment has been difficult on you," he says, and I nod against him. Then I look up, my eyes meeting his. "You can tell me more," he adds. "If you want."

And because no man has ever looked at me as he does—with such protectiveness, such care—I want to tell him everything. Instead, I settle for the dream.

"When I was younger, it was always me standing on the side of the road where my father crashed. I would have to watch him slamming on the brakes while the car kept speeding toward its violent end. Toward his end. And every time, just before I'd wake up, the whole scenario would slow down. As his car would wrap around the tree, I'd hear his voice telling me, 'Find the map, Eva. Find the map and save us all.'" I let out a nervous laugh. "That sounds ridiculous, right? The doctor who helped put the dream to rest convinced me that it was my own subconscious wanting to find a way to save my father."

Benedict tilts my chin up and brushes a soft kiss over each of my tear-soaked eyes.

"And now, angel?"

I steady myself. "Now it is almost the same dream, but it is Jasper behind the wheel and not my father. Yet the message has not changed, only the voice that makes the plea." I straighten in my prince's lap, more sure of myself than I've been for quite some time. "I think that doctor was wrong, or that maybe he didn't want me searching for whatever map this might be. Because I know my father was murdered. And I know my brother was set up. And if I don't figure this all out before they do—whoever they are—they will come for me next."

X clears his throat, and we both turn to where he stands in the doorway. X's jaw tightens. "Let me return to the library to continue my studies. I assure you that you and Miss Rub—Evangeline Vernazza—

are safe. I should have more concrete information for you by morning. For now, I think it best you stay with your guest."

Benedict opens his mouth to argue, but I interrupt.

"Please don't leave," I say to him. "If X can help, let him, but don't leave me alone here tonight."

He sighs and nods toward the doorway. "I will see you after my morning benediction, X. Meet me in the prayer room at ten. With answers."

X bows. "Yes, Your Highness." Then he dips his head toward me. "Rest well, Evangeline." And before I can thank him, he is out the door so quickly it's as if he was never there to begin with.

"How does he do that?" I ask. "It's like a magic trick."

Benedict laughs. "Just wait," he says. "I have seen him bypass doors altogether. Perhaps one day you will, too."

His tone is wistful, as if he speaks of a time in the future when our lives will still overlap, but I know this cannot be true as sure as I know that the way he holds me now is out of necessity, to wake me from the terror that threatens my sleep.

I swing my legs off his, but he does not let go of me.

"I'm sorry," I say. "This is most inappropriate. I should go clean myself up."

His only response is to dip his head toward mine and kiss me again. This time, though, there is nothing of the hunger from before. Just a sweet, gentle yearning as his tongue slips past my parted lips, as we both taste the lingering salt of my tears.

We lie down, his soft kisses continuing as we do. He pulls my body close and grins.

"What are you smiling at?" I ask.

"I didn't realize I could do that," he says. My brows pull together. "Kiss a woman," he continues, "and have it not be sexual in nature."

I stroke his cheek, my chest tightening at what it would be like to meet such a man under any other circumstances than the ones we are in. That's when I know I have to break this spell. I thought the hard part would be living with myself if I succeeded in tempting him from his holy path—or if I betrayed him to the Madam. I realize now the difficulty lies in thinking I could fall for such a man and not get my heart obliterated.

"I think I'm okay to sleep now," I say, trying not to sound too cold.

"Of course," he replies flatly, taking the hint, and I know I've hurt him…or at least bruised his ego.

He slides his arm out from beneath me and leaves the bed, lowering himself to the hard, wooden floor.

"Don't you want a pillow?" I ask. "Or a blanket?"

He rests his head on his forearm. "Not tonight. I must remind myself there are certain comforts that are not for me."

Like sleeping with a woman in my arms, I imagine him saying to himself.

Like believing a prince could choose you over God, I think, realizing my own guilty wish.

"Thank you for making me feel safe," I say, staring at the ceiling.

I hear him let out a long breath.

"You will always be safe with me, Evangeline."

Tomorrow morning we will find out what X knows of the map that must exist. Tomorrow night I will convince Benedict how dangerously tempting I really am—so that neither of us is seduced again into thinking there could ever be more.

So that my foolish heart understands there is no promise in a prince's kiss.

CHAPTER NINE

Benedict

NOT LONG AFTER she fell asleep last night, Evangeline cried out softly again. Another bad dream. Against my better judgment, I climbed in beside her, wrapping her trembling body in my arms and somehow silencing her whimpers. Her soft breaths must have lulled me to sleep before I could return to the floor.

Now, with the first morning light, I am warm, comfortable and unwilling to climb from the bed for a punishing cold shower and an hour of contemplation at my personal altar. Instead, I turn and find the reason still snoring lightly beside me.

In the soft light, devoid of her makeup, she is Evangeline. My blonde angel. My painting come to life—salvation and temptation all at once.

I can still taste the tender kiss we shared, the inkling that perhaps there is more inside me than animalistic lust.

Even now I don't want to ravish her. My cock twitches in disagreement, but my heart overrides the urges. Instead, I want to…take care of her.

I slide from the sheets with a reluctance that she

seems to echo as she emits a soft, purring moan of protest.

"Shh." I bend and kiss her forehead. She smiles dreamily and returns to peaceful sleep.

In my simple galley kitchen there is a used coffee mug in the sink. A sign X woke even before me and is already in the study poring over books, trying to get answers for Evangeline's many questions. I wonder, in fact, if the man slept at all.

There is time ahead to help her, to figure out if her dreams hold truth. But I am also convinced in the healing power of simple, kind gestures, like a fresh goat cheese and spinach omelet paired with thick slices of toast, the bread delivered fresh to the palace every morning.

I have always had a measure of talent when it comes to cooking, but food seemed like one more sinful pleasure, giving over to the body when I needed to focus on the spirit. So day after day I have eaten plain oatmeal for breakfast, a slice of whole wheat toast and a piece of soft cheese for lunch, and a simple root vegetable stew for dinner. It brings me joy to cut and dice these ingredients, put my larder to use to help plump Evangeline's cheeks, hollow from grief and fear.

When I return to the room holding a tray, she is sitting, rubbing her eyes. "Where did you go?" Her jaw falls open as she registers what I carry. "Oh."

"I thought you would enjoy breakfast in bed," I say, suddenly shy. What if she wants to be alone, just as she urged me out of the bed last night? Perhaps I am a fool to assume.

"I'm starving," she says, interrupting my inner

torment. "And this looks amazing. Like something out of a magazine or a reality cooking show."

"See if it tastes okay." I set it down and shove my hands into my pockets. "It's been a long time since I have prepared food for another."

She takes a bite and groans, the same sound I have heard her use when giving herself over to absolute pleasure. "This is wicked, Benedict."

Ice flows through my veins. "What do you mean?"

She bites her lower lip, eyes shining. "What is happening to my taste buds is a sin. I might require confession by the time I finish the toast."

I am unable to give voice to how much her small happiness brings me joy. So I offer her a soft smile.

She dips her fork into another bite, and this time her eyes roll. "I am serious. How do you know how to cook like this? I would think you'd have grown up with a hundred classically trained chefs waiting at your beck and call."

I nod. "This is true. But I was a curious child, also shyer than my brothers. I spent a lot of time in the palace library, which is even bigger than my collection here in the tower. I'd read everything I could get my hands on. Including cookbooks. Once Jean-Paul, the old royal chef, found me poring over a seventeenth-century collection of recipes from Versailles, and he invited me to the kitchen. It became my safe haven. I befriended the serving staff, the sous chefs, the pastry makers. They treated me as an equal, not as a prince or a future saint."

This is something I don't talk about, yet when I'm around her, my past spills out of me.

"It sounds like you have many happy memories from that time."

My smile fades. "Yes, until Father deemed it unseemly for a prince to perform what he believed were menial tasks."

She shakes her head. "But what you did here with food, it is art. No different than what I do with paint and canvas."

"I should like to see you paint someday."

She gives a wistful sigh, her fingers twitching as if holding an imaginary brush. "I miss it above all things. Except for, of course, Jasper and Papa." Her voice hitches.

"I'll tell you what." I clap my hands, inspiration striking. "Today you will do nothing but make art."

"But…" She is incredulous. "Aren't I supposed to be tempting you, giving you a taste of forbidden pleasure?"

"Forget all that. Your employ is only for the evenings," I say. "Let the days be your own. Besides, nothing would bring me more pleasure than seeing you happy," I say honestly.

She considers me for a long time before speaking. "You are a most unusual prince."

Another thought strikes, even as it causes me a glimmer of fear. "Of course, perhaps one bit of temptation before art."

"Yes?" I can see her eyes veil as she slips into her role of Ruby.

"On the roof of this tower, I have a claw-foot bathtub. It can only be heated by lighting a small fire beneath it. Normally I don't bother with it, but this morning, I want to give you a bubble bath. Wash your hair with fresh mountain spring water and watch as the sun rises over the peaks and turns to spun gold." I shall fill the tub with roses from the garden below.

"You are playing a dangerous game," she whispers, her hand rising to the side of her throat.

"How so?"

Her soft eyes gleam with a passionate intensity. "If you aren't careful, I might never leave your side."

Evangeline

Benedict leaves me to finish my delicious breakfast while he prepares the bath. My days are mine to do as I please, and as much as I know this will drag me deeper under his spell, I choose this. I choose to spend my time with him.

I'm practically licking the crumbs from my plate when he bursts through the apartment door, almost racing to where I still lie in bed. He wears nothing but a gray cotton T-shirt and the pants he slept in—and a sweet, boyish grin spread across his face. When I first saw him the other night, he seemed like such an old soul, but this morning he is youth incarnate, a young man with the world at his feet.

He dips his head. "Forgive me if I seem too eager, but I don't want the sun to make it past the mountaintops before we get up there. If you're still hungry—"

"I am beyond stuffed," I tell him, setting my plate on the night table. So he reaches for my hand, and I offer it without hesitation.

In seconds we are out the door and bounding up a smaller staircase around the corner from the spiraling one of which I've already grown quite fond. He

holds the door open at the top, and I step through to
see the entirety of Edenvale stretching out in every
direction, including the shimmering Royal River. I
race past the tub until I'm bellied up against a notch
in the tower's stone parapets.

"Oh, Benedict," I say, but I'm at a loss for words.
I may not have been born in this kingdom, but I
grow to love it more each day, despite the trials my
family has faced. I reach for Benedict but realize he
isn't there, turning to find him outside the door, back
against it, watching me from afar.

"Join me, Your Highness!" I call to him, teasing,
but he shakes his head.

Then he nods toward the tub, where I just now
notice rose petals floating atop the steaming water.

"Your bath chamber," he says with a grin, "is as
far as I go."

I give the landscape one more glance, the dawn
breaking across this beautiful kingdom, and make
my way to where he stands. This time I hold out my
hand for his, and he laces his strong fingers around
mine.

"I don't need any of this, Benedict."

"But you deserve it," he says. "You deserve a
bright and beautiful morning after such a dark night.
To bear witness to your happiness is enough for me."

I swallow the threat of tears and place my palm on
his cheek. He was so good to me last night, taking me
in when I had nowhere to go, soothing me from my
nightmares. And the only thanks I gave him was to
practically toss him out of bed and to the floor when
all I wanted was to slumber in his arms.

He presses a soft kiss against my hand, and a ripple of warmth spreads from his lips to my very core.

Benedict leads me to the tub, where embers of kindling still glow beneath it.

"I will douse the remnants of the fire if it's too hot."

I dip a finger into the gorgeous copper tub, a fixture most definitely fit for royalty, and shake my head. "It's perfect." I lift the silk gown over my head, baring myself to him, and to my surprise, he does not react with shock. His eyes, green pools glowing in the ever-increasing morning light, look upon me with a reverence I have not seen before. Without a word, he holds my hand, guiding me into the fragrant warmth, and I lower myself until I'm covered in ruby-red petals of the sweetest roses I've ever smelled.

I hum softly as I try to convince myself this isn't a dream.

"I don't need to see what lies beyond the walls of the roof," he says. "Not when I have the most beautiful view of all of Edenvale right here. Just for me."

He kneels next to me and takes off his shirt, his taut muscles rippling in the glint of the rising sun. I run my fingers atop the dusting of dark hair on his chest, and he sucks in a breath.

"I'm sorry," I say, letting instinct overpower logic. "I didn't mean—"

"Don't apologize for putting action to your desires. You have the freedom to do so. I only wish I had the same."

He dips his head toward mine and kisses me. I taste the bitterness of coffee, delicious on his tongue, emboldening me to wrap my arms around his neck, tugging him closer. Water and rose petals slosh over the lip of the tub, soaking his pants.

I let him go, and we both laugh, the sound of his happiness something I have not heard before.

"Sorry!" I cry, my hand flying to my mouth as I only laugh harder. "This is all just a lot—the roof, the roses, the most beautiful man I've ever seen kissing me at sunrise. I'm a little out of my element, and I guess I got carried away."

His laughter subsides, and he collects himself. "Most beautiful man you've ever seen?"

I touch him on the shoulder, on his very muscular, naked shoulder. "Now you're going to tell me you don't read the papers or watch TV." He arches a brow. "Okay, fine. You probably don't watch television because it's pleasurable, and I get it. Deny, deny, deny. But come on, Benedict. Despite your holy calling, the women in this kingdom are mad for you."

"Ah," he says, leaning back on his heels. "So I am some sort of celebrity fantasy to you?"

I roll my eyes and groan. "No. I mean, yes. You are beautiful to look at, but two days ago that meant nothing more to me than having a pleasurable view while I tried to seduce you."

"And now?" he asks with a wry smile. "Everything has changed in a mere thirty-six hours?"

Impossible, I think. But yes.

I rest my hand on his chest and let his heart beat against my palm for several long seconds.

"So much of your beauty lies in here," I say. "And I'm honored to be one of the few who get to see it."

He stands, staring at the pants that are soaked

against his long legs. Then he shrugs and steps over the lip of the tub, lowering himself in across from me.

I yelp with laughter. "What are you doing?"

He reaches over the edge for a copper pitcher and fills it with the rose-infused water.

"I'm going to wash your hair."

He scoots forward, his legs crossing over mine. Water sloshes over the edge, spilling onto the roof, and I swear I've never felt happier.

He pours the pitcher over my head, then massages my scalp with hands that are strong and full of purpose. Yet I also feel a gentleness in his touch, one I've not experienced since the days when my father was alive.

"What about shampoo?" I ask, even as I moan with pleasure.

"These roses are from the palace garden," he says. "There is nothing softer or more beautiful than the aroma of their perfume. I've also added some essential oils to the water, which will soothe and nourish your scalp."

I tilt my head into the cradle of his hands and sigh, the tension of last night evaporating with the steam.

"Benedict," I say softly.

"Yes?" His hand caresses my cheek.

"Thank you for holding me this morning." His eyes widen. "I remember the nightmare starting again, and I know it was you who chased it away. It's okay," I assure him as I watch his eyes turn dark with worry. "I'm glad you were there."

"You're welcome," he says, his voice hoarse.

"Come," I say, grabbing his shoulders and urging

him to turn around. The welts on his back have gone down, but angry bruises remain. I kiss each one before pulling him to me, his back against my breasts, his head cradled against my shoulder. "Let someone hold you for once."

I kiss his temple, and he nods. Without another word, we lie there together, watching the sun crest over the snowcapped peaks. I'm certain we would have stayed there all day, or at least until the water was too cold to bear. Instead, just as the whole roof is bathed in the morning glow, I hear the door burst open behind us.

"Highness!" X calls. "I've found the map."

CHAPTER TEN

Benedict

EVANGELINE IS NESTLED in an oversize leather chair in the library. Her freshly washed hair streams over her shoulders. Her small feet poke from the bottom of my bathrobe. The red paint is chipped on her left big toe. Something about the sight is endearing, yet I can't explain why.

X clears his throat, an understated reminder of why he called us in from the tower roof. Even now my pulse pounds, making it hard to focus on the easel dramatically covered by a white sheet.

"You have our attention," I observe wryly. "Now on with the show."

He ignores my verbal poke and turns to Evangeline. "I have reason to believe that beneath this sheet is the reason why your father was murdered and your brother, Jasper, was taken prisoner." X pulls away the sheet and there is my painting of my guardian angel.

A confused silence follows.

"I was gifted this piece by my brother Nikolai last year for Christmas. He respects my interest in art collection even if he doesn't share the passion."

"Nikolai didn't realize what he was buying you—it is beyond the value of money," X says. "There are people who'd stop at nothing to own this piece."

"It is priceless," I answer. In less than a month I will take my final vows. This portrait of a younger Evangeline will be my reminder that our time together ever occurred.

X clicks his tongue in irritation. I've never seen him like this, as if reaching the edge of his legendary composure. "My sources have learned that Jasper, Evangeline's brother, intentionally sold it to Nikolai. We think it was intentional, to keep the piece from falling into the wrong hands. He must have decided that the well-protected walls of Edenvale Palace would make the perfect hiding place."

Evangeline rises and pads across the room, her mouth creasing in a small frown.

"My God. Look!" Her hand flies to her mouth. "The necklace."

"Yes!" X exclaims. "Yes, exactly. You see what I mean!"

"It cannot be," she says. "It's a legend."

X's face is dark with repressed emotion. "Is it?"

"Do you two mind speaking plainly?" I rise and join them. The image is the same one that I've seen on my wall a thousand times. A sad-eyed ethereal beauty rising above the wasteland of a terrified populace fleeing a handsome young man.

"The angel is wearing a necklace with a vial. A vial of golden water," Evangeline says slowly. "Look, it's there, half-hidden amid the folds in her robe."

"Golden water?" I chuckle. "From what? The Spring of Youth? That's an old story. Surely if there were such mineral compounds in nature that could keep a person looking young while prolonging life, they would have been patented by major American pharmaceutical companies. They would be worth billions, if not trillions of dollars to a society devoted to worshipping youthful beauty."

The fabled Spring of Youth was said to exist beneath Edenvale in a cavern deep beneath the earth. The specific combination of minerals were said to delay the effects of aging, but it came with a price— whoever drank the elixir would live longer but slowly lose their mental faculties, descending into paranoia and madness.

"Edenvale is a land of ancient secrets. Perhaps this artwork provides a rare answer," X says.

Evangeline touches the corner of the painting. "Father loved symbology. Look at the street signs— Detour and This Way. The angel also raises two fingers. I had always assumed it was in benediction, but it could also be read as—"

"A sign of The Order." X's expression is deadly serious.

"The Order?" I frown at their excited faces. "As in the Knights of The Order?" They cannot be serious. "The secret society of legend?"

"Charged with protecting the realm. The best knights of Edenvale once vied to be selected for the honor. This painting somehow links to The Order and provides a key to the map. But how?" Evangeline speaks almost to herself.

I feel as if we are discussing the existence of Santa Claus or the Easter Bunny. "The Order hasn't existed since the Dark Ages."

"Some say the members have gone underground," X says gravely. "Secretly protecting the realm to this day."

"From what?" I ask. "Magical water?" I would think he was teasing me except for the fact his lips don't twitch.

X nods at the dystopian landscape, the violence. "That." His tone deepens with a strange intensity. "To live on young and beautiful, even with the threat of madness? Many despots would be tempted by such an opportunity."

Evangeline blinks. "My father is hiding something here behind the canvas. If only I had something sharp to open it in the back…"

"Like this?" X pulls a four-inch steel blade from his trouser pocket, the edge sharpened to deadly perfection.

Evangeline's mouth opens, then closes. I chuckle and shake my head.

"Do not try to make sense of a man such as X," I say, then turn my gaze to the man himself. "Nikolai needed a bodyguard with all his public escapades. I'm not sure I need protection from anything at all, but it's good to know that if I do, you're more than prepared."

Evangeline clears her throat. "Perfect." She reaches for the blade and raises her brows in a quizzical expression. "May I?"

"It would be an honor to watch Vernazza's daughter at this moment." X's voice is grave.

She slides the knife along the back of the frame. Her movements are quick and assured. At last she pauses, wipes her forehead. "Here goes nothing."

Peeling back the paper, she reveals what I never could have fathomed—a map written in black ink, the paper yellow with age…and in the center is a symbol of a spring, and written beneath it in gold leaf script are the words *aquas vitam aeternam*.

"Waters of Eternal Life," I translate.

Evangeline

"Waters of Eternal Life." Tears spill from my eyes, but I'm careful not to let the salt water drip onto the map. Benedict has his prayer books, but this—for me—is the most sacred of texts.

"Oh, Papa," I say, my fingers carefully skimming the parchment. "What did you die to protect?"

A warm hand caresses my shoulder, and Benedict presses a soft kiss on top of my head. I want to turn to him, to bury my face in his chest, but I'm transfixed by the vision before me. An angel, ageless faces and the key.

"It's like losing him all over again," I say, sniffling. I run the sleeve of Benedict's plush bathrobe across my eyes. "And now to know that I'm not crazy, that this wasn't all some terrible nightmare that has plagued me for a decade…" I spin to face both of them now. "It's real, right?"

X nods, and Benedict runs his fingers through my hair.

"Realer than real," he echoes, but my prince's words are not a question.

"What now?" I ask.

X takes a step forward and carefully pulls the map from the frame.

"Well," he says, brows raised as he holds the map out for all of us to see.

I squint at the lines of text above a map that leads who knows where. "Are those even letters?"

"It looks more like code," Benedict says.

X shakes his head. "In all my linguistic studies, I've come across this but once. Were it in Portuguese or Uzbek, I'd have had this translated before you finished peeling back the painting. But this—this will take some time."

I nod, but I cannot hide my disappointment or the new wave of tears it brings.

"So that map is real," I say, "but we don't know where it leads or what my father and brother were protecting?"

What does the Madam want with this map? Or worse—who is she working for? I've heard many whispers of her connection to Nightgardin, Edenvale's centuries-old enemy.

It's up to me now to protect what my father sacrificed his life for. I must protect the wonderful, caring prince who's been protecting me, which means keeping this map to the legendary Spring of Youth from falling into the wrong hands.

X bows his head toward Benedict. "Your Highness, I can decipher this code. It may take a few days, but it can be done. Take Miss Ruby—I mean, Evangeline—to your brother's old quarters in the palace. I do believe both of you will be safer within its fortified walls."

The prince scoffs. "The tower has never been breached."

"This is no time for pride, Highness. You may not think you need protecting, but she does."

He nods and snakes his fingers through mine. "You're right. We will head to the palace at once."

He squeezes my hand and starts to lead me from the library, but I stop in my tracks.

"My family," I say. "Jasper's wife and daughter. They could be in danger, too."

All Benedict has to do is give X a look, and the other man nods.

"We will send men from the Palace Guard to keep watch."

This is enough to satisfy me. Benedict retrieves a coat from his chambers and throws it over my shoulders before I finally let Benedict lead me away. By the time we get to the future king's annex, the one where he lived before he and Kate married, all of my belongings from the cottage are already there.

I call Camille to check in and breathe out a sigh of relief when I hear her voice.

"I think we can help Jasper," I tell her. "Maybe even free him."

She gasps. "But—how?"

"I can't say too much right now, but know that the prince and his guard are helping us, and we will have Jasper home soon. Just promise me you and Lola will lie low until I call again in a couple of days, and speak nothing of this to anyone. I love you both."

She agrees, and I decide not to tell her about the guards being sent over, since I don't want to frighten her. They'll be there, surrounding their apartment building but hidden, looking after her and Lola, and that's what's important.

When I end the call, I notice I'm standing alone in the annex's kitchen, that Benedict has given me privacy to tend to my family matters. I swallow the knot in my throat and send a message to the Madam.

Haven't found it yet, but the prince and I are growing closer. He's beginning to trust me. I should have what you need soon.

The response is immediate.

I am growing impatient, girl. If I find out you're lying, you'll have more to worry about than me marring that pretty face of yours. I have very influential friends. It won't take much for me to get to the people you care about.

I wrap myself tightly in the oversize coat, breathing in Benedict's scent as I realize the gravity of my lies—that one misstep could mean Jasper's life... or my own.

I take off the coat and pad down the hall to what I know will be a lavish bedchamber compared to Benedict's, but what I'm greeted with is far beyond my expectations.

My hand flies to my mouth, and Benedict grins.

"I thought maybe this would help get your mind off the map for a bit."

He stands next to an easel, a blank canvas leaning against it, and beside it, a table full of paints.

"How?" I ask. It's more than what he's given me. It's that his gift is exactly what I need right now. How can this stranger somehow know me so well?

He shrugs. "The palace does have its perks. It's simply been a long while since I've wanted to take advantage of them."

I stride toward him and don't even hesitate when I wrap him in my arms and squeeze.

"Thank you," I whisper into his chest. "Thank you, Benedict."

He stands frozen before pulling me in even tighter.

"Anything for you, angel," he says, and for the moment, I actually believe it.

I look up at him, his eyes an enchanted forest of green.

"But I don't want to paint the canvas," I say, and his brows draw together. "I want to paint what I see in your eyes—paint you."

He says nothing as he removes his T-shirt, baring his chest to me.

"You have not put your collar on since the other night," I say.

He shakes his head.

"And this is okay?" I ask, reaching for a tube of green paint and squeezing it onto a palette. I dip a brush in, swirling it around, and then bring it to his chest, where I paint one single leaf.

Still no words, but he nods, backing toward the four-poster bed.

"But the linens," I say.

"Fuck the linens."

He lowers himself to a ruby-red duvet.

I gather the colors of my forest onto the palette and lay it on the bed. Then I climb over him, brush in hand, parting my robe so I can straddle his legs.

He is hard beneath his pants, and I...I am bare

but for the material draped over me, on fire for my prince, for this man.

"Stop me if it's too much," I say, and he grabs my wrist.

"Paint first. Then I'm going to tell you what I would do to you if I could." He unties the robe completely, letting it fall off my shoulders. "How many times I've looked at that painting, wondering if such beauty truly existed in the world. Now here you are. An angel in disguise. In another time, Evangeline—"

"Don't," I say, swiping the brush across his jaw. "Just for today. Please. Don't talk about what we can't have. Instead, let us enjoy what we can."

He nods and reaches for my breast, cupping it gently in his palm. He gives my peaked nipple a soft pinch, and I writhe against his hard cock.

"Benedict."

I feel him flex against me.

"It's not a sin," he growls, squeezing his eyes shut.

I drop the brush on the palette, then lean over and kiss him, the paint on his jaw smearing against mine.

"You're still just a man, Benedict. This is your choice. I won't take anything you are not willing to give."

His hand slides along my torso, skimming over my belly, and resting between my legs. He stills for several seconds, time lengthening between us. And then, there it is, the tiniest of movements—his thumb brushing my clit—but it's enough to make me cry out.

"I—" he says, his deep voice hoarse with need. "I want to know what I'm missing."

Then he slips a finger inside me, and I'm certain that I see stars.

CHAPTER ELEVEN

Benedict

I'VE FOUND HEAVEN on earth. It is tight, wet and perfect. My index finger has been inside Evangeline's pussy for only a few seconds, but it's as if I've lived five hundred lifetimes in the span of each one. When I start to withdraw, my fingertip slides over a small ridge near her entrance.

"Oh God!" Her inner muscles clamp as her neck arches. Her skin is so delicate that her veins are visible, her pulse rapid-fire fast.

Ah, the infamous G-spot. So it does exist.

My answering groan tears the fabric of my soul. I'm not meant to touch. But now that I am here, it feels holy to give her the pleasure she craves. I crook my finger and smile as her lids flutter.

"Benedict," she murmurs, hips undulating. "My God, Benedict."

"Your mouth was made for one thing," I growl, flipping her and bending over her.

"What's that?" She squeaks on the last word as I stroke her hidden secret again.

"Saying my name." I slip in another finger and still another.

"Yes, feels so good," she purrs, taking hold of my forearm, urging me to drill deeper. "Fill me. Fill me up."

"But this is too much." I pause and try to hold on to a shred of sanity. "I don't want to hurt you."

Our gazes lock and her pupils are dilated so much that I can see my own reflection in their onyx depths. "This is incredible."

"You're so tight." The walls of her tunnel are like slick satin. "I had no idea it would be this tight."

I brush her G-spot again and hold it as she mewls.

"Yes, there, don't stop. Don't ever stop, Benedict." Her pussy clamps my fingers, milking my hand with her orgasm, and I am humbled to my bones by this unexpected gift.

I've given a woman the gift of pleasure, and not just any woman, but one who is conquering my mind, body and soul. I have overcome my years of hard-earned repression and done the forbidden, and what's more? I've fucking loved every second of it.

As I move to withdraw, she frowns. "Don't go."

I have heard of this, a woman's ability to keep attaining pleasure. "You want to come again?"

She hums a sexy laugh. "All day if I can. You're quite talented, Highness. Your fingers are very... nimble."

"Must be all those years I spent kneading bread."

But her laughter ceases at my attempted joke. Instead, she looks hesitant.

"What is it?" I murmur. "Don't hide. You know you can tell me anything."

"The other night, you asked me to touch myself and tell you my fantasy. I didn't know until I cried out your name that you had somehow infiltrated my dreams. And now that I trust you—now that I know you'd never do anything to hurt me—I want something more."

My eyes widen. "I am part of your fantasy?" I ask.

She nods. "I've never asked this of anyone, but…" She trails off, and I nod, offering her encouragement to continue. "I…I wonder if you'd be willing to try something." She pushes an errant lock of hair off her cheek and nibbles her plump lower lip. "Something that I have never done before with any man."

"What?" I rasp, my throat threatening to clamp shut.

"I want to feel your whole hand inside me."

I freeze. "I…I am not sure that I understand."

Her cheeks are the color of flame. "I'm sorry. I know I shouldn't have asked. It's just that I feel so connected to you, and I've always had this fantasy but have never trusted anyone enough to give it to me."

"You truly want this?"

She gives a hesitant nod. "As you can see, I am not…loose. My vagina is incredibly tight, so the pressure feels amazing. Most women can't get off from penis-to-vagina sex."

I nod. "Yes, I've read about this. They need clitoral stimulation."

"Exactly. And while I enjoy such stimulation, I can come without it…if my partner is able and willing. I realized as a younger girl… Oh my gosh, I can't believe that I am telling you this…" She trails off.

"Evangeline, nothing you say could ever shock me. Your body is made to feel pleasure, to have desires. You can trust me."

She stares at me as she worries her bottom lip between her teeth. "I know I can. At first I thought it was because you were an old soul, but now I wonder if it's due to something deeper." She covers her face with her hands. "I feel—oh God, don't laugh—but I feel as if our souls recognize each other."

I let out a long, shaky breath. "You are saying we are soul mates?" With a few words, she has moved the rock long crushing my heart. At last, real heat pumps through my cold veins, returning me to life. I've become a flesh-and-blood man…with a man's needs.

"You want me to put my entire hand in your pussy, to fist you." My thumb twitches at the idea of giving her such depraved pleasure.

She peers through her fingers. "I have heard other girls at my…work…say it can bring about the most intense pleasure. But it is not something to do with a paying client. The trust factor is huge. You must open yourself up to another in the most intimate way possible."

I remind myself that, while I am at a precipice, taking the leap will still leave my own virtue intact. It is a selfish rationalization, but it is one that comforts me nonetheless.

"I will do what you ask," I say after a considered pause. "Except I don't have lube. As wet as you are, I would be required to exert a great deal of pressure and couldn't bear the thought of giving you any pain."

"A little pain can be a pleasure." Dark lust flashes in her eyes. "But I appreciate your consideration. I happen to have a bottle of lube with me in my red suitcase there on the chair across the room."

I arch a brow. "You travel with lube?"

She arches one right back. "This is my job, Benedict," she reminds me, a truth I've tried to bury. "And part of the Madam's requirements is that we are prepared with whatever a client might need. I travel with a great deal of lube, and a host of flavors: pineapple, raspberry or cinnamon." She dips her head, looking up at me through hooded lids. "I've also been told this type of...creativity...can also serve as a diversion, interesting a man in something more playful than..." She trails off, then sets her gaze on me directly. "You aren't like the others would be, Benedict. I am sure of it. I trust you...with everything."

I rise and cross the room, open the suitcase and select a small unscented vial that promises warming sensations and guarantees to delight. I slather my entire hand until it's well coated. It seems so big, and she is so tight. Three fingers felt like I'd packed her full. But I take my place next to her on the bed again. If she trusts me, then I will trust what she desires.

"Thank you," she says in a quiet voice. "For not judging me. I felt a little silly admitting this fantasy to you. But this isn't something I wanted to ever share with a client, only a man I knew would treat me with care, who'd fill me with a loving touch."

"Never apologize for wanting what you want." There is a small wet sound as I slide my fingers in. "I've read about this."

"Of course you have." She offers a sweet, teasing smile. But as I fill her, her hands grip the sheets.

"The word itself sounds fast and hard, but in reality it requires patience and a great deal of arousal," I say.

Her mouth forms a perfect O. "We have both of those factors on our side."

"Relax," I tell her. "You are in charge of the situation." I press my thumb beneath my four fingers to make my hand as narrow as possible. "If you need me to stop at any time, for any reason, I want you to tell me."

"Yes. Yes." Her thighs tremble.

I go slow, and the knuckles are the trickiest part. She takes deep, measured breaths, urging me on, then with a slight rotation of my wrist over her pubic bone, I'm all the way inside, my hand naturally forming a fist. Her muscular walls quiver around me.

"How do you feel?" I whisper.

"Vulnerable," she breathes. "Impossibly full. Stretched to my limits. I'm close. So close, Benedict."

With my free hand, I lick my fingers and circle her clit. It takes the barest whiff of pressure, and she reacts with tidal force, bearing down on my enclosed hand with an orgasm that threatens to cut off my circulation. I continue to worship her clit, letting her ride through two, then three orgasms.

They can probably hear us from the guard towers to the servants' quarters, but nothing, including the Big Man himself, could make me stop.

"Benedict," she squeaks, toes curling, as she grabs a handful of hair. "I never knew. I never knew it could be like this. So full. So good."

My heart threatens to burst. "Neither did I, angel. Neither did I."

Evangeline

We lie there in silence, me coming down from a high I never thought possible, and Benedict beside me, his jaw tight and body anything but relaxed.

Both of us are staring at the ceiling when I ask, "Benedict?"

"Angel," he responds, and I smile at his use of my nickname. At least what just happened hasn't changed that.

"Please tell me you are not quietly chastising yourself. If I've made you feel guilty in any way, I won't be able to forgive myself."

He props himself up on an elbow and faces me, the hand that gave me pleasure like I've never known now tracing lazy circles around my belly button.

He kisses my temple. "Guilt?" he whispers. "Surprisingly, no. I've been trying to figure out how to put a voice to what I have decided. More so, I hope it will not be too much to ask of you."

I take his wrist and guide his hand from my torso to my breast. Still, after what I've just asked of him, this elicits from him a ragged moan.

"Let me do something for you," I say. "Trust me like I trust you."

He rubs a thumb over my raised peak, and I gasp.

"I know where this road will lead me," he says. "What awaits me at the end of this path."

I swallow. "Your vows," I say, realizing that a tiny part of me had the nerve to hope that whatever he is going to ask of me might involve some sort of future for us beyond the end of our month together.

"Yes. My vows. My vows are my future—but you said something before that hit me." My brows rise, and he continues. "Right now?" He rolls my nipple between his thumb and forefinger, and I let out a soft moan. "Right now I am just a man."

I prop myself up so we are eye to eye. "What are you saying, Benedict? Do you want to…?"

"God can have my virtue," he says. "But you, Evangeline, you can have everything else."

It is not the answer I was hoping for, but it's close enough. I slide closer to him and let my fingers tickle the flesh above his pants.

"May I have this patch of skin?" I ask, itching to follow the trail of dark hair to where it leads.

"You may," he says with a grin, and I dare to keep traveling south, beneath the seam of his cotton pants—where there is no undergarment for me to tease any further.

He's right there, within my reach. All I have to do is stretch my pinkie, and then I feel it—the warm, slick precum on his tip.

Benedict lets loose a growl.

"This, my prince. Is this mine? Does this fall under everything else?"

"Yes," he says through gritted teeth, and I know that today will be a day for many firsts.

And that's all it takes for me to slide my hand the rest of the way, to wrap my hand around his thick, hard length and stroke him from root to tip.

"Evangeline!" He bucks against my touch, his reaction making my pulse quicken.

I climb over him, tugging his pants to his ankles and then off completely.

I gaze upon his naked form, speechless for a few erratic beats of my heart.

"What is it?" he asks, and I shake my head.

"You're…quite the specimen," I say, feeling a rush of heat from my core to my cheeks. "To think that this will be hidden away forever…and that I am the only one who will have seen it? Why me?"

The corner of his mouth curls into a grin that lights a fire within me.

"Because you are the most exquisite soul I've ever known."

My breath catches. "You don't know my soul, Benedict. You couldn't possibly. This—" I motion between us "—this is fantasy. This is two strangers giving each other what they need." I have to say this because to believe otherwise is too much. To believe otherwise is to want what I could never have.

He grips his cock, tilting it toward me so his wet tip slides against my clit.

I hiss, exhaling in a sharp breath. "Benedict!" He does it again, and I shudder.

"You said our souls recognize each other," he says. "Then believe that it's more than recognition— that I know yours. That I know *you*." He caresses my cheek. "This is not fantasy," he says. "It is me giving you everything I possibly can before it is no longer mine to give."

I drop over him, sliding along his length until that naughty tip nudges me again. He clamps his jaw shut, groaning as I writhe. This man—he may be preserving his virtue, but he will drive us both mad in the process.

He slips two fingers inside me, and I sink down to his knuckles, pretending it's his cock filling me instead. I imagine taking him so deep, forgetting where I end and he begins.

I manage to maneuver my body while he vibrates within my walls, so that now his cock is in front of me, and I lick my lips before sucking him down to the base.

"Fuck!" he cries out as I grip him, my hand trailing my mouth as I slide up his long, slick length. Again and again I do this, and he answers by adding a third finger, by fucking me the only way I think he can until he slides his hand free and replaces it with his mouth.

His tongue is warm, lapping between my folds, and I am a lit fuse about to explode.

I cup his balls and squeeze, all the while bucking against him as his tongue swirls around my throbbing clit.

I said I didn't need this to come. But I never said it couldn't take me to the edge of the universe. That he couldn't take me there. Because he can, as will I for him.

"Fuck!" he cries again as I start to tip over the edge. "God. Evangeline." But he loses his words completely, exploding inside me, and I drink him in. Every last drop. Because this is the only way we will ever be as one, and I want to savor the taste of him, the intimacy, the knowledge that while his seed will never grow inside another, I am nourished by it nonetheless.

I collapse, and he rises to his knees.

"You're not finished," he says.

I shake my head.

"Good. Because I need to taste the nectar of the gods one more time."

"Gods?" I ask, raising a brow. "Why, Benedict, I believe that's blasphemy."

He pushes my knees apart and gives me a wicked grin.

"Then forgive me, Father, for I'm about to make this angel take your name in vain."

He drops between my legs, and though I do cry out for God in heaven, I do not think it is in vain. Instead, it is a prayer...or maybe a plea.

Let this man remain just a man. Let him have all that he's denied himself. Let him find happiness where he wishes to seek it and not where he's been told to find it.

And then I add on one selfish request.

Let him be mine.

CHAPTER TWELVE

Benedict

FOR THE NEXT WEEK, I barely make it out of bed, except to take quick showers. I enjoy all manner of delights off Evangeline's delectable body: greenhouse strawberries covered in lashings of whipped cream, a drizzle of wild clover honey, dark sea salt chocolate. Once I've devoured my fill, I feast on her instead. The sweetness between her legs puts even the most gourmet Belgian chocolatiers to shame.

This morning we are still in bed even though the sun is nearly at the sky's apex. Her small foot nestles between my hands, and I give her a massage with almond and cherry scented oils. Another of my angel's secret delights? Getting her feet rubbed.

And here's one of mine—I love giving her exactly what she loves.

I'm riding a dopamine high, satiated physically, and even more important, experiencing true intimacy with a woman for the first time in my life.

"What are you looking at, Highness?" she asks, coyly circling one of her rosy nipples. The unselfconsciously sexy action sends a shock wave through my core.

"Why, I'm looking at you, angel."

I increase my pressure, kneading the ball of her foot. Her lids flutter in a sort of ecstasy. I love that my touch brings her joy on so many levels, from carnally depraved acts to these gentle moments of tenderness. In fact, this is what surprises me most. I never doubted that physical pleasure with another would be anything less than addictive and amazing. But it's these quiet interludes where we aren't sucking and mouth-fucking, grinding and groping, that make me happiest.

I could watch Evangeline sit naked and cross-legged on the bed all day—doing nothing but sipping Earl Grey and sketching me—and consider myself contented.

She has filled almost an entire notebook with my nude form.

I'm not sure what she'll do with it when she eventually leaves. I stiffen, my jaw tight as always when I think of such impossibilities as our eventual separation. I am arrogant enough to assume that she will take my images with her and on some lonely night in the future look at them with a smile playing on her lips of the sweet time we shared, these magic hours when the world seemed to stop for us.

We haven't taken things all the way. Christ, I smirk at myself. I sound like an earnest virgin.

But if the shoe fits…

I'm a virgin who has fucked a woman with his whole hand, allowed her to trace her tongue over every acre of my cock, kissed her from her aroused clit to her rosebud ass.

But I have not truly entered her.

Nor will I.

For as real as this feels, we still are playing a game of pretend. And for all intents and purposes, I am her client. No matter what emotions I think are tugging at my heart, I hired her from that Rosegate madam to be mine for a month.

If I enter her now, one thing is for certain…I won't ever be able to fulfill my destiny. If we join together, we will never be put asunder.

So I hold back, and though it seems to disappoint her, I have made sure to make it up to her in other ways that cause her immeasurable pleasure—and multiple orgasms. My current record is five in one session.

And it's one that I'm determined to break.

"What shall we do this afternoon, Your Highness?" she asks idly.

"I was thinking of trying that trick with my tongue that made you claw at my shoulders like a she-cat," I answer with a studied nonchalance.

She tosses a pillow at me, laughing. "A she-cat."

I point at the claw marks on my shoulders. "Do you have a better description?"

"I plead innocent," she says, opening her eyes extra-wide for emphasis. "I was driven out of my mind by lust."

"I'll drive you out of your mind," I cry and lunge at her, hooking her around the waist and tickling beneath her ribs.

There's a knock at the door.

"Did you order room service?" I ask, willing to let her go if she is famished. We've kept up quite the athletic horizontal routine.

"No, you?"

I frown. "No."

The knock sounds again with increased urgency, and I get the sinking feeling that our happy time here sequestered from the world has come to an abrupt end.

Evangeline lets out a huff of annoyance and wiggles into a pink silk nightshirt crumpled beside her. I get up and wrap a towel around my waist, sauntering to the door. It's a disappointment but not a surprise to see X there, hands clasped, face serious.

"I apologize for disrupting you, but this couldn't wait."

X has been hard at work deciphering the language of the map. What he thought would take him a mere day or two has lasted the week.

"Of course." I beckon him forward. "One moment so that I can get decent."

I duck into the bathroom, where I tug on a pair of sweatpants. My chest is covered in love bites. It turns out Evangeline likes to mark her territory, and for the time being, she considers my body hers.

I love seeing them there, a reminder of some of the happiest times in my life thus far.

When I come out, X is still standing, and Evangeline kneels on the edge of the bed covered in my robe.

"I couldn't get him to crack," she says. "He refuses to tell me a single word."

"That's because I didn't want to share this information without Benedict close by to provide support." X's voice is calm, cool, but also kind.

"What does that mean?" Evangeline rises up off her knees, her cheeks blanching with alarm. "Oh my God, Jasper. He's not... He isn't... Oh no, no, no—"

"No, not Jasper. Your sister-in-law, Camille, has been arrested, and your niece, Lola, has been removed to a government-run orphanage."

Evangeline

I crumple into a ball on the bed, convulsing with sobs. Here I've been basking in pleasure for the better part of almost two weeks, as if in denial of the danger my family still faced. Whoever started this has already taken from me my father and my brother. Now a mother and her child? Who could be so hateful? So merciless?

"Shh, angel. It will be okay," Benedict whispers as he rubs my spine.

I can barely speak through the tears. "This is my fault," I tell him. "I came here to do a job—to earn enough money to take care of them. To save my brother. Maybe I have been doing this for them, but I've also been indulging my every fantasy." I nearly choke on a hiccuping breath. "Because of my selfish whims, my niece—" I can't bear to think of it. "Oh, Lola," I cry. "Why didn't Camille call me? Prisoners are allowed a phone call, aren't they?"

X shakes his head. "This place is...different."

Benedict continues to try to soothe me, but I push him away, scrambling off the bed to where X stands.

"I have to help Camille—and get Lola out of that place!" I tell him. "You can help, X. I know you can."

He swallows but just stands there. Then I feel Benedict's hands on my shoulders.

"Evangeline," he says. "Of course X can help. We both can. But this is beyond our jurisdiction. The mother…she is imprisoned in Rosegate, yes?"

My whole body trembles as I nod.

"Your Highness," X says. "Despite our years of diplomacy with our territory, we have no direct oversight of their courts or laws. This is part of the Rosegate Compact of 1702."

I learned about this in primary school as a child. Our small kingdom was a simple city, smaller than Monaco and more akin to Vatican City, a country once walled off from the rest of Europe, with a focus on pleasure-making and the arts. At last, feeling the looming threat of war from the aggressive Nightgardin, Rosegate gave up much of our independence to be protected by Edenvale—but not all. And we never lost pride in who we were, a cultured people with a storied history.

"And, of course, the fact that last year your brother spurned the Baron of Rosegate's sister and blew up their planned engagement means we can't go through any direct route," X adds.

Through puffy eyes, I watch a silent conversation transpire between my prince and his guard. Benedict narrows his eyes at X, his jaw set in quiet obstinace.

"Your Highness," X says again, but nothing comes after.

For a long, drawn-out beat, neither man says a

word. Benedict simply stares the other man down until X finally grumbles something.

"What was that, X?" Benedict asks with the authority of a true royal.

X crosses his suit-clad arms. "It was Sanskrit. I'm afraid the true meaning of my sentiment will get lost in translation. But if you are determined to try your dealings with Rosegate in this matter, then I must assist you."

I throw my arms around X's neck and kiss the man's cheek. "Thank you!" I cry. "Thank you! Thank you!"

Then I turn to Benedict, and he looks at me with a measured gaze.

"I have not forgotten our arrangement," he says, his voice calm. "I have sent two weeks' worth of payment to The Jewel Box already—and I've put some extra in a private account for you to access once you leave this place."

The muscle in his jaw ticks, and I want to reach for him, to assure him that as much as I need the money, he has become so much more than an assignment. But I can't lose focus again. So when my fingers twitch, and my hand begins to move, I stop myself before I can feel his stubble against my palm.

"Thank you" is all I say. "I'm going to clean myself up. Then have to leave for Rosegate at once."

Benedict is quiet for much of the three-hour ride to Edenvale's neighboring territory—to the place I truly call home. Though in the back of the Rolls-Royce that X drives, the prince sits with my hand in his, every now and then giving me a gentle squeeze to let me know he is still there.

I've gotten so used to seeing him in plain clothes—or nothing at all—that to see him in the habit of a priest once again is so jarring that I wonder if the man sitting next to me is the same one who has tasted every inch of my body.

"This is who I am," he says softly when he notices me staring.

I nod, and my throat tightens. "But is it who you want to be?"

"Evangeline," he says, but nothing comes after the utterance of my name.

And I get it. He has a duty to fulfill, whether he wants to or not. It is the way of his family, and despite his carnal needs, Benedict Lorentz is a man of honor. We are so much alike, the two of us. Bound to family in a way that choices seem to be made *for* us rather than of our own free will.

"This sure as hell isn't who I wanted to be," I say, forcing a laugh. But he doesn't respond. "I'm not proud, you know. Of what I have to do to take care of the ones I love." I swipe at a tear under my eye. "But there aren't many options for me in the art community at the moment, not with our family name being dragged through the mud like it is. It's funny, though. If the other girls knew I was a *prince's* whore—"

"Stop!" he growls. He drops my hand and grabs me by the shoulders. I see the pain in Benedict's dark green eyes, and I know that I've hurt him somehow.

"Never, Evangeline. Never do I want you to call yourself such a name again. Do you understand me?"

I open my mouth to answer, but he doesn't wait for me to do so.

"That account I set up for you—it's not just for the month you'll be with me. It is to take care of you and your family after we go our separate ways. I will not send you back to that place. I will not let another man—"

This time I interrupt him.

"I am not yours to save," I say, though I know I'm a hypocrite. Here we are, entering the city of my birth, where I'm fully willing to let him leverage his power as a priest to get what I need. Because the truth is, if anyone could rescue me from the life I never wanted, it would be this man.

I would choose him. But he can't choose me.

"Highness, we are here," X says over the intercom, and I look out the window to see a sign that reads Rosegate Institution for Female Confinement.

Benedict and X both convinced me that trying to see Jasper is too risky. With me being the only one to solve this puzzle and save my family, whoever is after us—and I know the Madam fits in here somewhere—cannot know that I've found the map.

But a recently imprisoned woman who has called upon her personal priest for confession...

Benedict is our ticket to Camille.

"Do you remember the plan?" X asks, and Benedict nods.

"How can you be sure they will not recognize me?" the prince asks.

X lowers the partition and turns to us, grinning. "Because your brother is the face of Edenvale right now, and while I know living in his shadow might be unpleasant at times, you will now use it to your advantage. It would be wholly unexpected for Edenvale royalty to walk into this institution unannounced—and that is precisely why it will work."

I raise my brows, my gaze volleying between the two men.

"X," I say, "you speak as if you do this kind of thing all the time."

He winks. "I assure you I do nothing of the sort, Miss Evangeline." Then he turns to Benedict again. "They have a chapel on the premises. That is where they will bring her to meet you. It's imperative that you take her to the confessionals on the second floor. Should anything go wrong and you have to abort the mission early, there is a zip line that runs from the second-story window straight over the outer stone wall. We'll pick you up there if necessary."

Benedict squints at something in the far-off distance. "Do you mean that wall out there with the barbed wire at the top?"

X nods. "That's the one."

"And I'd have to jump out of a second-story window to attempt traveling over that wall?"

X nods again. "Yes, exactly."

"And if I ask how there came to be a zip line from the chapel to the property beyond the prison?" Benedict asks.

X gives him a crooked grin. "I'm afraid I'm not at liberty to divulge that information."

Benedict clears his throat. "Well, then. Nothing will go wrong," he says.

He kisses me quickly and exits the vehicle.

CHAPTER THIRTEEN

Benedict

"Father John?" A weasel-faced guard frowns at the roster. "I don't seem to have you here on my list of approved visitors."

"I arrived at the Rosegate Monastery last week." My tone is mild but firm, velvet stretched over steel.

"From Edenvale?" The guard cocks a brow and scratches the side of his pointy nose.

My accent gives me away as expected. I keep my face a gentle mask, the model of a simple priest come to hear prisoner confessions. "Yes, I'm here in your lovely city on a sabbatical."

The guard grumbles under his breath but seems reluctant to grill a man of the cloth.

"On your way," he mutters, hitting a buzzer that allows me entrance, and picks up a pornographic magazine.

Charming.

I pass through the thick stone walls topped with barbed wire. No woman has ever broken out of a Rosegate prison and lived to tell the tale. X must have been joking with his talk of zip lines. Despite

Rosegate's reputation as a city of beauty, art and learning, it has a dark underbelly, not unlike many old European cities. In this case, it's home to an old, but notorious, penitentiary.

A grim-faced female warden greets me with a downturned mouth. "Morning, Father. This is an unexpected visit."

I give her the sign of the cross. My hand does not betray me with a tremble. My features remain as calm as with the guard out front.

"There is no right or wrong time to find succor in the mercy of the Holy Spirit," I say mildly.

She snorts and flexes her large fists. She looks like the sort of person who drowns puppies for fun. A steely-eyed woman for a coldhearted place. The air is sour with hopelessness, as if those behind the bars have been abandoned by God Himself. Through one of the barred windows high above comes the unsettling sound of sobbing.

"No one has signed up to hear confession in weeks," she growls. "Besides, what good will it do 'em?"

From somewhere deep inside the prison bowels comes a terrified scream. "No, please! No!" It's cut off with an abruptness that makes my throat tighten.

"For those who are of the faith, the sacrament is an opportunity for atonement, to cleanse the soul from the stain of sin." It's all I can do to steady myself in the face of so much casual cruelty.

"Ha! Hope you've come armed with bleach and industrial cleaner to deal with this filth." She whirls and sees a female prisoner scurrying past clutching a stack of books. "You there, where are you going?"

The woman flinches as if expecting to be struck with the billy club hooked to the guard's utility belt. "I'm Prisoner 35495, assigned library duty."

"Well, I don't like the look of you, 35495," the matron snarls. "What was your crime against the city?"

The woman bobs in an awkward curtsy. Her cheeks are gaunt. It looks as if she hasn't eaten a proper meal in months. I feel sick to my soul. This is what passes for justice in these parts? I'm part of the royal family and therefore culpable in this mistreatment. Rosegate might be a special city with special rules, but prisoner mistreatment is a violation of international law.

"Begging your pardon, miss," the woman stutters, her Rosegate accent making me wince. She sounds so much like Evangeline, who is now outside, waiting for me to send word of her sister-in-law's fate. "I'm a pirate."

"But there's no ocean near Rosegate. If you take me as a fool, I'll show you who laughs last around here." The warden's eyes are slits as her hand, the one that reads hate, slinks to the club.

"Begging your pardon again, I mean no disrespect," the prisoner says hastily. "See, I was convicted of piracy, not with regards to the ocean or ships, but for stealing." She hangs her head, her grimy face stained with shame. "I pirated a great deal of intellectual property. Books, to be specific. Hundreds if not thousands of them. That is why I work in the library now. I only have another month on my sentence, and I am trying to atone for the error of my ways."

The warden looks flabbergasted anyone would

steal an item such as books. "Be gone from my sight, worm," she commands. "Now, where was I? Oh, you…" She looks at me as if I'm dog excrement stuck to her combat boots. "Like I said, no one signed up for confession. Sorry you hiked your holy butt out from the monastery, but we can't help you none."

I think fast. "But surely you have new prisoners. My monastery informed me that your new intake occurred this week." The lie flows so smoothly off my tongue that I almost convince myself.

She eyes me warily. "What's it to you?"

I'm setting off her internal alarms. "New prisoners might not have time to have requested confession."

She shrugs. "We only got one this week. Treason."

I don't blink an eye. "Then it sounds like she must have much to unburden. If you would be so good as to show me the way to the chapel, I'll wait for her there."

The warden blinks but finally grabs her radio. "Main Yard to Solitary, Main Yard to Solitary."

There is a crackle over the walkie-talkie. "This is Solitary, over."

"Yeah, I have a priest here who needs to hear the confession for the new prisoner you have on the floor."

"Prisoner 54329?"

"That's our girl."

"She started a hunger strike. She might be weak."

The warden's smile chills my blood. It is a promise of torture and cruelty untold. "Tell her to get moving or I'll drag her out myself…by that long ponytail of hers. She is scum, just like her thieving husband."

"Copy. She will be sent to the chapel. Over."

The warden smacks her fleshy lips with satisfaction. "You do-gooders don't know. These people are criminals. You have to treat them with a heavy hand. Fear is what will save them in the end. Not love."

I draw myself to my full height and allow a glimmer of my royal arrogance to gleam through my eyes. "That's enough."

She gasps and takes a few hurried steps back. "These lives, Father. They don't matter."

"I disagree," I say firmly. "Now take me to the chapel."

Evangeline

I pace outside the car while X leans against the front bumper, relaxed as if the prince sneaking into prison—unrecognized—is something that happens every day. Every few paces I stop and glance up at the stone wall that must be twenty feet high, the menacing barbed wire tracing the perimeter.

"Do you really have a zip line set for Benedict to escape if need be?" I ask.

X nods.

"How? This place is a secure fortress. And you didn't even know we were coming here until you walked into the annex this morning."

The man merely straightens his tie. "*You* didn't know we were coming here until I walked into the annex this morning."

My mouth opens and closes as I try to decide whether or not he is playing me. "You know heights are not his favorite, right?" I ask, sounding like a petulant child. Though it's not X who is deserving of my chastisement. I am. Because if anything happens to Benedict, it will be because of his involvement with me.

X simply nods again. "It is amazing what one can overcome when he has no choice but to face his demons."

I cross my arms and set my jaw. "Haven't enough choices been taken from him?"

X raises a brow, like he knows that my desire for Benedict to choose his own path is sprinkled with my own selfish hope.

Just then a crackling sound comes from the open window of the Rolls-Royce.

"What was that?"

He grins.

"That, Miss Evangeline, is our royal highness, Prince Benedict."

I run to the window and peek inside. "Did you tap into some sort of internal audio system?" I ask, expecting to see computer equipment that would alert me to X's possible hacking abilities, but all I find is a fancy digital watch sitting on the dashboard. I brandish it toward X. When my eyes meet his again, he takes the watch, fastens it to his wrist and shakes his head.

"A bug," he says, and I swat at the air around my head.

"Where?" I ask. "Is it a wasp? I think I might be allergic." My eyes dart from side to side looking for the would-be attacker. X steps around the nose of the car and grabs the hand that tries to shoo away the invisible insect.

"Not that kind of bug, Evangeline." He points to the watch. "This kind of bug."

"You have five minutes," a faint but distasteful voice speaks. "Then this one can get back to starving herself."

Someone makes a soft grunt, and then I hear him speak.

"Are you ready to make your confession, my child?"

It's Benedict, loud and clear. But it's the next voice that stops my heart.

"Forgive me, Father, for I have sinned. It has been…a long time since my last confession. I've done many things, told white lies, taken the Lord's name in vain, been envious of other people. But you have to believe me that I'm innocent of any crimes that have landed me in this godforsaken hellhole." She gasps. "Forgive me again, Father. But someone is trying to hurt my husband and is now using me to do it. And our girl…" The woman sobs softly, her words muffled but understandable just the same. "They have taken everything from us. Just, please, find my darling girl."

"Camille!" I cry, but X covers my mouth with his strong hand.

"Listen," he whispers. "But do not call out, for either of them. Do you understand, Evangeline?"

I nod, trying to calm myself. But I cannot, not after I hear the desperation in my sister-in-law's words, not now that this is all too real. Jasper. Camille. Lola. Even Papa. They've all been taken from me, punished one by one, all for some stupid map

hidden behind my painted face. A painting I was
sent to find—one I may now give my life to protect.

"What if I said I could take you to her?" Benedict
asks, and my whole being stills. What is he talking
about? We came to talk to Camille, to find out what
happened to get her locked up. Benedict couldn't
possibly have the means to do what he's offering.

"Then you would be more powerful than God
himself," Camille says. "I have prayed, begged, be-
seeched the Lord with my pleas to save my daughter,
but I see no way out of this horrid place."

"Not out," Benedict says. "Over."

My eyes widen. Benedict went in there alone, but
he plans to come out with Camille.

"I'm going to remove my hand now," X says.
"That is, if you think you can behave."

I nod again, and he steps away, lowering his palm
from my mouth.

"He came here to get her out?" I ask softly. "We
came here to save her? Is this why there's a zip line?"

The corner of X's mouth quirks into a devilish
grin.

"How can you possibly smile at a time like—"

But X isn't listening to me. Instead, he brings his
wrist to his mouth, touches something on the watch
and then speaks to it.

"Now, Highness! Grab the girl and get out of that
place at once!"

I hear Camille yelp, and almost immediately after,
shouts ring out across the prison yard.

"There's a jumper at the chapel!"

"Prison break!"

"Is that a…flying priest?"

"Holy shit. Sound the alarms!"

And then the alarms do sound. Just as quickly I hear a whistling and whirring noise, which is when I notice the nearly invisible line that skates over the sharpened wire that follows the perimeter atop the wall.

"They aren't going to make it!" I cry, caring nothing for the volume of my voice at this point.

"Get in the car!" X cries, forcing me toward my door. "Now! Now! Now!"

He throws open the door and hurtles me inside. I barely have time to right myself before we are careening away from the prison wall.

"What are you doing?" I scream, frantically clawing at the glass partition. "You can't leave them!"

My hand is on the door handle, and I'm ready to throw it open, to tuck and roll and run back to do…I don't know what! I am helpless to save Benedict and Camille, just as I was helpless to save my father. My brother.

X slams on the brakes hard. I'm thrown from my seat and onto the floor of the vehicle. I scramble for the door, but it opens before I can get to it. There stands my prince, dusting off his priestly habit with one hand, his other entwined with Camille's.

"Eva!" Camille cries when she sees me.

"Highness, we must get to the safe house. My associate will meet us there with the child."

Benedict helps my shell-shocked sister-in-law into the car, and she hiccups on a sob. "Evangeline…did he just say 'the child'? Does he mean my Lola?"

As soon as everyone is in the car, X races off again.

"He does, miss," Benedict answers her question.

"Wait, I know you." Camille's eyes bug out of her head. "I thought you looked familiar in the prison. But it can't be... Am I dreaming? Has that terrible prison made me mad already?"

"You're safe. Just breathe." I grab her hand and give her a warm squeeze. "But how?" I ask my lover. "Did you know? I mean, I thought we were only going to get information."

Benedict shrugs. "This is X's doing, angel. All I knew was that eventually I'd have to jump. The rest is X's secret to reveal."

But the man behind the wheel stays silent, so I wrap my brother's wife in a hug and squeeze as I whisper, "I'm sorry," over and over again.

Then I check both her and Benedict for any barbed wire–related injuries and see nothing to give me pause until I find a tear in Benedict's pants above his outer thigh, blood staining the edges of the fabric.

"You're hurt," I say, my throat tightening.

"I'll live."

Then I launch myself into his arms and kiss him hard.

Camille gasps, and Benedict smiles against my lips.

"Camille Vernazza," I say, "meet Benedict Lorentz, Prince of Edenvale."

CHAPTER FOURTEEN

Benedict

"WE'VE GOT COMPANY," X says grimly, interrupting the family reunion taking place in the back seat of the Rolls.

A squadron of sirens fills the air. I twist around, my gaze narrowing. A dozen patrol units are in hot pursuit, speeding up the steep mountain switchback below. If I had any illusions they were hoping to bring us in for questioning, it's shattered when a flurry of gunshots erupt in staccato pops.

"Get down!" I fly over Evangeline and Camille, shielding them with my body. Dull metallic thuds shudder through the car as bullets riddle the bumper.

"I've never heard of law enforcement behaving in such a way," Evangeline breathes. Her body trembles, sending my protective instincts into hyperdrive. There is nothing—no damn thing—that I wouldn't do to keep this woman safe and free from suffering. My body would happily endure any torments, as long as she makes it through this ordeal alive.

"Law enforcement would never act in this fashion," X snaps.

"These thugs are going through a hell of a lot of trouble trying to appear as rank-and-file police officers. The sirens are an especially authentic touch. But no." His voice hardens. "There is nothing legal about the men pursuing us. They are here for one thing and one thing alone. The map to the Spring. And they will stop at nothing until it is in their possession."

Evangeline grips her now sobbing sister-in-law.

"This is all my fault! We'll be caught for sure." Her eyes, sheened with her own tears, meet mine over the top of Camille's head. "I'm so sorry for dragging you into my mess. My brother and I are cursed. We hurt everyone we come in contact with and—"

"Don't say that!" Camille cries. "Your brother is a hero to Rosegate—"

"Hold on." X takes a bend at over one hundred and thirty kilometers an hour.

Jesus Christ, he isn't breaking a sweat.

Who is this guy?

Evangeline brushes an errant strand of hair. "The danger that you're all facing is because—"

"Of our choosing," Camille interrupts. "I knew what your brother was before I agreed to marry him."

"What?" Evangeline's laugh is incredulous. "A mild-mannered art historian? What danger did you think he'd get you into? A narcoleptic state where he waxed on for five hours on the birth of French Classicism or inquiries into Gothic architecture?"

Camille's brows smash together. "But surely you know."

"She doesn't," X says in a steady voice, increasing the speed as he pushes the throttle into fourth gear. "Evangeline hasn't been informed of a great many things. Her brother and father left her in the dark, hoping to keep her safe. I'm sad to say it's had the opposite effect."

Outside the Rolls's windows, the mountain wild-flowers blur into a single hue of pinkish purple. The engine hums. We're going too fast. There's no way we can hope to take the next turn.

Sweat prickles my chest. X meets my eyes in the rearview mirror. He silently asks for my trust. The sirens grow louder. My brother Nikolai trusted this man with his life day after day, and also the life of his true love. Now I must do the same. I give a single curt nod, and I swear the man smiles.

"Your brother? Mild-mannered?" Camille gives me a disbelieving laugh. "You really don't know!"

"Know whaaaaaaaaaaa!" Evangeline cries out as X misses the next turn altogether and flies straight off the asphalt.

My stomach turns in a sickening somersault as the Rolls soars through space. No one screams. The two women must be in shock, because there is only stillness. It reminds me of the time I flew in a glider with Damien and Nikolai, back when we were three brothers united by love and laughter.

The sirens fade behind us, but below a mournful whistle cuts through the valley.

A train.

"Excellent." X checks his watch. "The 5:55 express from Geneva is running right on time."

"You can't be serious," I say as the Rolls descends faster and faster. Outside my window a bird of prey soars past and does a double take.

"Serious is my middle name." X grips the wheel. "I've timed it perfectly. Everyone stay calm, and— that's it, really. Just stay calm."

A twelve-car commuter train stretches out beneath us.

"You've done this before?" I shout.

A small muscle in his jaw twitches. "Of course not! Who'd be insane enough to drive a Rolls-Royce off a mountain and try to land on a moving train?"

The next three seconds go fast and slow all at the same fucking time. I feel as if I live a thousand lifetimes in fear, not for myself but for the woman beside me. She's going to survive this no matter what happens. There's a thump and X slams the brakes.

We are balanced in the center of the car.

He dusts off his shoulders. "Well, I have good news and bad news."

"After the stunt you pulled, I'll take the good first, thanks," I snap, fighting to keep my heart in my chest.

"We're alive."

"That is always a bonus," I comment wryly. "Now for the bad news."

"We're about to go into the St. Georges Tunnel." He gestures to the looming black hole in front of us. "I'm afraid that the Rolls is lost. A pity. I love this car."

Evangeline and Camille grip each other tightly.

"The train will slow going into the tunnel." I go into hyper-focus. "We'll need to jump."

"Yes." X doesn't hesitate because we are obviously out of time. "An unconventional but necessary outcome, I'm afraid, Highness."

"Jump?" Camille moans. "We'll break our necks. I'm going to leave Lola an orphan."

The whistle blows as the engine car disappears into the mountain tunnel. The train begins to drop in speed.

"Here's what we'll do." I'm utterly calm, my protective instincts taking over. Nothing bad will happen to Evangeline. I will do whatever it takes to see her safe. "Stay loose. Fear makes you tense. If you stay relaxed, you'll have a better chance of not being injured."

Evangeline gives me a surprised look.

"Before I was in the seminary, I was a black belt student of jujitsu. I even trained in Brazil for a summer. We learned how to fall properly through hours of relentless practice."

X nods. "Yes. Good advice. We're going to all jump off the left side."

"The key will be to land on the balls of your feet, press your knees together and keep your chin tucked at all costs," I order. "When you hit, twist so that your calves and thighs hit the ground before your head and shoulders."

Evangeline is shaking as Camille hyperventilates.

"There is no choice. The tunnel is here!"

Evangeline

"Now!" X cries, and before I can react, he throws the driver's-side door open and leaps from the vehicle.

Tears stream down my face as I look at Camille. "Go!" I say. "You must get to Lola!"

She nods, and Benedict flings open the door. She

doesn't look back—scared as I know she is—and jumps.

A strange silence holds Benedict and I suspended in this final moment. Logically, I know that the train's engine alone is deafening, but my world has boiled down into his eyes.

"I'm not leaving you," I say with a sob.

His green eyes shine as he forces a smile. "We cannot jump together, angel. It is too dangerous. You must go first." He takes my hand and squeezes it. "If I could give my heart to any other than God, Evangeline, I would give it to you. Whatever happens, know that this was never about what I hired you for, not after that first night."

I open my mouth to say something in response, but the whistle blows violently, the final alarm.

"Jump!" he cries, and as I hurl myself from the door, I whisper words he cannot hear.

"I love you, my sweet prince."

I try to remember Benedict's directions as the ground speeds up to greet me, as I hear the sickening crash of metal hitting the tunnel walls—the Rolls.

Balls of my feet, bend my knees, twist. But I twist the wrong way, and I cry out as something feels like it snapped in my knee. The pain makes me gag.

I roll, my limbs now tucked to my chest as my cheeks scrape against branches strewn across the small clearing in the woods. When I finally stop moving, I lie there for a minute or two catching my breath, checking myself for any other injuries. I touch my cheek, and my fingertips come away with a light smear of blood. But everything else seems intact.

That is, until I stand, forgetting about the whole knee-twisting-on-impact incident.

I crumple to the ground again and hiss from the gut-twisting agony, but I cannot stay here. Once whoever is chasing us finds the wreckage from the Rolls—and doesn't find us wrecked inside it—they'll know we escaped.

So I crawl to my feet, balancing on my left leg while I attempt to put the slightest bit of weight on my right. It hurts like nothing I've ever felt before, but I'm able to limp, slowly. I cross my fingers that it's just a sprain and hobble in the direction of where the tunnel opens, which I know will eventually lead to a main road. We had no time to discuss where we would all meet after the jump, so I assume this is my next logical move.

I want to call for Benedict, Camille or X—not just because I'm afraid to be alone out here but because I need to know that they're okay—but if whoever is after us is already searching the woods, that is the last thing I should do.

So I limp for the tracks, gritting my teeth each time I put pressure on my right leg. This is the only way I'll find Benedict again.

It feels like a lifetime when I finally make it to a road, but there is no one there to greet me. I can't walk any farther, though, and am about to collapse when I hear the faint rumble of a car's engine. If X had this whole prison break planned, then he must have foreseen us needing alternate transportation.

Adrenaline courses through my veins, and I'm filled with a renewed sense of hope when a black limousine with tinted windows rolls to a stop where I stand.

"Benedict!" Happy tears fall as the rear door flies open. But my elation turns to horror when a woman I don't recognize steps from the vehicle. She is sturdy and strong with an unforgiving sneer on her face and a billy club in her utility belt. She raises a brow and gives me a studied gaze, that sneer morphing into a terrifying smile. She cracks her knuckles, and I read the words *love* and *hate* tattooed across the fingers on each hand.

Without a word, she backhands me across the face, on the already split-open cheek, and my teeth clatter. I cry out and stumble. But she catches me by the wrist before my knee gives out, her steely grip nearly pulling my shoulder from its socket.

"Get inside, whore. Madam would like to have a little word."

That voice. I've heard it. I swear it is the same one I heard speaking to Benedict inside the prison, but there is no time to ask questions.

She jerks my arm, and I pitch forward into the vehicle, my hands and knees bracing my fall as I hit the floor. Stars dance across my vision, and I think I might be sick, but my attacker follows me in, hauling me onto the seat before my body has a chance to react. She yanks my hair so I'm facing my employer, a woman I know only as the Madam.

Once the limousine door is closed, the Madam removes her black hat and with it the short, netted veil that covers her face. She is frightening and beautiful at the same time, with her porcelain skin, jet-black waves falling over her shoulders and lips as red as blood. She stares at me with eyes so dark I almost think they are black, but I decide I must be hallucinating from the pain.

"Ruby, Ruby, Ruby," she lilts in a soft voice that could lull me to sleep if I didn't fear for my life. "You were hired to do a job, and so far you have failed."

She smiles, her lips curling to reveal perfect white teeth.

My captor gives my hair a swift tug. "This is the part where you ask what you can do to make it up to the Madam," she says in a gruff tone.

I swallow hard. "I...I thought you would be pleased with the new arrangement," I say. "The prince is sure his brother only meant for me to tempt him for the night. Now I have the rest of the month to find—"

The Madam cuts me off with a terrifying laugh. "Prince Benedict still thinks his brother, the future king, brought you to him? Then he's more naive than I thought. Yes, Prince Nikolai is the one who requested Pearl. But that simply gave me my in to use you."

"He tripled my fee—" I start, but I almost choke when my head jerks again.

"You're done speaking until I say," the other woman says.

The Madam is impatient. "This was never about money, sweet jewel," she says, then leans forward to caress my cheek with an icy finger. "It was about trust. I knew that prince would never be able to resist another reluctant sinner. Now that he's risked his life for you—and dare I say fallen in love—we have our trust." She brushes her hand across my bruised and bloodied cheek, and I wince. "Stop. Wasting. My. Time. I know you've found it. But that's no longer enough. Bring me the map, Evangeline, and your family will suffer no more."

She knew. This whole time she knew that painting was me—that it belonged to my family.

I grit my teeth, even as I tremble. "Never," I say, and the brute of a woman next to me threatens to scalp me with her grip. "I will not betray him."

There has to be another way.

The Madam sighs, pulls a phone from a clutch beside her on the seat and hands it to me.

"Just press Play," she says, and with a trembling finger, I do.

What I see is worse than any nightmare that has plagued me for the past ten years. It is my brother, Jasper, tied to a chair as someone dressed head to toe in black, an executioner of sorts, punches him again and again in the face until all I can see is blood where his eyes should be. I hear the horrifying crack of what must be his nose breaking, and I shriek when the person in black removes a dagger from their boot and holds it to my brother's neck.

But Jasper doesn't say a word. I cannot even tell if he is conscious. But he was at some point. He took that beating without making a sound, and I realize this is not the quiet, reserved man I know. This is a man with a strength I never knew he possessed, strength these people are trying to test, but he does not give in. And just as it looks as if I'm about to watch my brother's murder, I hear the Madam's unmistakable voice say, "That will be enough."

The screen goes black.

I tremble, barely able to speak. "Did you... Did you kill him?" I stammer.

"Not yet," she says with measured calm. "He claimed not to know where the map was, but thanks to your correspondence with dear Camille, we realized that you do."

Camille's phone. They've been listening to our conversations the whole time.

"But I never said—"

The Madam waves me off. "You said enough for me to know that you already have what I need and have the audacity to think that you can stall for more time. The Order can't stop us now. Simply bring it to me, and all of this goes away." She reaches for the phone still clutched in my hand. "And if you disappoint me again? Well, let's say that the police guard outside your brother's hospital room can be easily persuaded to turn a blind eye while we finish the job." Her lips part into a bloodred smile. "And remember— if we can get to you in your little royal residence, we can get to your prince, too." She leans close, her breath caressing my cheek, and my body convulses. "Imagine the pious second son found murdered in his chamber by his filthy whore. Think of what that would do to his family—to his memory."

I shake violently, but I won't beg this monster for mercy. I already saw what she did to my brother. I have no doubt in her threat—at how easily she could end Benedict's life and point the finger at me. And though I'd never raise a violent hand to my prince, his life is in danger because of me. I would, in essence, be his killer.

The Madam places the veiled hat back on her head and nods to the woman next to me.

"You get to return to your prince now," the other woman says with one final tug at my hair. "If you know what's good for you—and your friends—you won't breathe a word of our little encounter. And at midnight tonight, you'll bring the map and anything else you've learned to that sweet little fairy-tale cottage of yours. One of our people will meet you there to collect it."

She throws open the door and steps out, grabbing my wrist and forcing me to follow.

"I know you won't disappoint the Madam again," she says.

When she lets go of my hand, I crumple to the ground, my strength and my resolve flooding out of me all at once. The tires crackle as the car rolls away, and I squeeze my eyes shut trying to erase the vision of my brother sitting in that chair, broken but unwavering in his purpose of protecting the location of the map.

And now I have to betray him—and the man I love—to save them all.

"Evangeline!" I hear in the distance, but I decide it must be a dream, so I keep my eyes shut.

I don't want to wake up now, because the nightmare doesn't just exist when I sleep. "Evangeline!"

"Benedict?" I whisper, but it's too late. Pain, exhaustion and fear pull me under as strong, sturdy arms scoop me up, my head cradled into a warm chest.

"It's okay, angel," he says. "You're safe."

But we're not. We never were. So I'll do what I
have to do to save Jasper's life—to save all of them—
even if it means losing Benedict for good.

CHAPTER FIFTEEN

Benedict

"BENEDICT, BENEDICT. Is it really you?" Evangeline burrows deeper into my chest, murmuring my name over and over like a prayer.

"I am here, angel." I kiss the top of her head, inhaling her sweet scent. "I'm right here. Everything is going to be all right. We're back together."

"No!" She gasps. "Nothing is ever going to be all right ever again!" Her eyes are unfocused. Her cheekbones have been slashed by brambles, and there's a sickening bruise on one temple. "The whole world feels on fire. All dreams nothing but fire and ash." And with that her body goes limp as the darkness again consumes her.

A crow calls somewhere deep in the forest. I shudder. In our country, the crow is an omen of death and dying.

I step off the road in favor of the tree cove, my feet padding the detritus fallen from the towering pines. The air is thick with sap warming in the dappled shafts of sunlight slicing through the ancient branches. This place feels primeval, beyond time and almost holy.

A branch cracks, and a frisson of awareness skims my skin. We are not alone.

I turn, ready to fight to protect the beautiful woman who lies unconscious in my arms.

"X!" My shoulders slump at the sight of my guard. "Jesus Christ, am I glad to see you."

He raises a brow, the man looking relaxed and ready for a night on the town, no worse for the wear after jumping from a speeding train. "Thought you weren't supposed to commit blasphemy."

I narrow my gaze. "Today I have busted a woman out of prison via zip line, taken part in a high-speed chase in a luxury vehicle and held on as said car broke through guard rails and landed on top of a commuter train. Oh, and then I jumped off that train to avoid being decapitated by a mountain tunnel. I believe the Holy Spirit is willing to cut me some slack given the circumstances."

X's broad shoulders shake with a rumble of soft laughter as he passes a hand over the top of his head, removing a stray pinecone. "Fair enough."

"Two questions," I say. "How do you look as if you've merely been out on a stroll, and where is Camille?"

X ignores the first question and answers the second. "Camille has been picked up by friends from The Order. She will be taken to a safe house while we attempt to locate the daughter in the orphanage."

Evangeline gasps.

My eyes widen. The men and women of shadow.

Secret assassins and ancient defenders of the secrets of our realm.

"You heard a crow earlier. That was the signal she had been located. The crow is their symbol."

"The symbol of death?"

"For their enemies. And also themselves. They must kill off the parts that know fear."

I glance through the underbrush. Are these secret soldiers watching us even now?

"It is just us here," X says, cuing into my thoughts. "No easy solution like a safe house for a member of the royal blood, I am afraid. But not to worry. Help is on the way—or at least will be once I fetch the chopper."

"A helicopter?"

X cracks his neck. "My apologies, Highness, but there isn't time to explain. Four hundred meters down the hill you will run into a stream. Follow it for a kilometer, and at the junction look up. You will see a small cave. It is one that hermit monks once used as a shelter to avoid the temptations of the world. You will find it stocked with medical supplies to tend to Evangeline, food and a warm bed. Look to the west when the last light of the sun falls. I will come for you. You and Evangeline will be safe within the palace walls well before midnight."

Evangeline

I bolt upright in bed and cry out, my cheek burning with pain. A hand reaches for me, and I swat it away, expecting to see the word *hate* tattooed across knuckles about to make contact with my skin.

"Evangeline!"

I'm not strong enough to fight him off as his hand wraps around my wrist, and that's when my vision clears. I'm not being held captive in that limousine anymore.

"Benedict," I say, and I stop struggling. "I wasn't dreaming."

He shakes his head, but his emerald eyes are a storm of worry. "You're okay, angel. But I think the jump was the hardest on you."

He reaches gingerly for my face with his other hand, a hand that holds a cotton swab doused in some sort of liquid.

"I thought I could clean the wound while you were unconscious, that I could spare you the pain. I'm sorry to have startled you."

Even though I know it's coming now, I still wince.

He pauses. "You took quite a beating out there," he says with a forced smile.

I close my eyes and nod, bracing myself for the sting. With it comes the reminder of what really did happen out there—and that I cannot tell him any of it.

I take a shuddering breath as he swipes the cotton across my skin. Tears stream from the corners of my closed eyes, and almost as quickly as they begin, I feel Benedict's lips kissing them away.

"I'm sorry," he whispers. "I'm so sorry." He drops the cotton onto a tray beside the bed.

I blink and take in my surroundings, realizing we are not at the palace.

"What is this place?" I ask, voice trembling.

"Where are we? Are they still looking for us? What… what about Camille? And X?"

"Shh," he whispers. "We're safe. X led us here, and he'll return this evening to take us home. Camille is on her way to be reunited with Lola. Everyone is okay."

Benedict tucks my hair behind my ear and swipes at a falling tear. I exhale, daring to let my shoulders relax.

"Everyone's okay?" I ask, remembering the one person who isn't.

Jasper.

He nods, but his brows pull together. "I thought—" His mouth clamps shut, the muscle pulsing along his jaw. "I thought I might lose you," he says, his voice rough.

You will, I think, and swallow a sob. It is the last thing I want and yet the only way to make sure Jasper lives. That all of us do.

"I'm right here," I say, because whatever time we have left together, I want to give him my full attention—to give him whatever he needs. Because despite what must happen when we get to the palace, I love him.

I slide back to rest against the headboard of the bed, hissing as I put pressure on my leg.

"What is it?" he asks, his eyes wide with alarm.

"My knee," I tell him. "I twisted it when I landed."

He pulls away the blanket. "Jesus," he whispers. "You need help. The swelling is bad."

I nod. "I know. And did you just take the Lord's name in vain?" I ask, trying to smile.

He lets out a bitter laugh. "Yes. And it's not the

first time today." He moves to the button on my jeans, and I gasp.

"What…what are you doing?"

He continues his movement as he speaks, pulling down my zipper. "I grew up with two brothers," he says. "I know enough about sprains and breaks to be able to determine how serious the injury is. I'm not sure how to get X here with the helicopter any quicker, but if we need to get you to a hospital, we'll find a way."

"No!" I cry, knowing that if I don't complete my task tonight that Jasper may not be alive tomorrow. "No hospitals—not until we know they're not looking for us anymore." The lie comes so easily, but I know to tell him any of this would be to risk his life as well as my brother's.

I cooperate, though, as he tugs my pants over my hips and to my ankles. He must have already removed my shoes, because a second later my jeans are on the cave floor.

His brows pull together, and he rests a warm hand on my knee. I squeeze my eyes shut, too scared to look.

Benedict's relief is in his voice. "Nothing looks out of alignment." I open one eye to peek at him… and at the swelling. "Can you bend it?"

I slide my heel just enough to raise my knee off the bed, biting the inside of my cheek to keep from crying out. But I can move it. That has to be a good sign.

He leans over and kisses the bruised skin. "It needs ice," he says against me. "We won't be able to tell much more until the swelling goes down, and

I worry that we won't be able to tend to it for some time."

I touch his face, his stubble scratching my palm, and finally let the tiniest bit of relief flood through me.

"I thought I'd lost you, too," I tell him. "You made sure everyone else got out of the car first. We were so close to the tunnel. I didn't think there was enough time—"

He crawls up beside me and kisses me, soft at first and then with a fierceness that tells me that whatever's been happening between us this past week, we've crossed over a threshold today, and I'm not sure we can go back.

"I'm right here," he says, echoing what I said to him.

"I know." He kisses me again and again, each one hungrier than the last. "But I feel like I can't get close enough—like I cannot satisfy this need to keep you safe. I don't want to let you out of my sight again."

My hands cradle his face as our lips meet once more. Our tongues tangle and dance, and I know what he means. Because I pull him closer, kiss him deeper, but it's not enough.

He lifts his head, his chest heaving, and his gaze bores into mine.

"What's wrong?" I ask.

"I don't want to hurt you."

I skim my hand along his temple. "I don't feel any pain when you're kissing me," I say.

He shakes his head. "That's not what I mean." He takes in a long, measured breath, then lets it out. "I want to tell you something, but I'm afraid that in the long run, all it will do is hurt you. Hurt both of us."

And because I know what he wants to say, I decide to relieve him of his burden and say it first. To let him know that it's okay. To follow his destiny, he must break my heart. And for me to protect the ones I love, I must also break his.

So I beat him to the punch.

"I love you, Benedict." His eyes widen. "I love you, and whatever happens after this, it's okay. I'll survive it."

I watch his Adam's apple bob as he swallows. Then he grasps for the hem of my shirt, lifting it over my head.

"I love you, Evangeline. With every beat of my traitorous heart. With every shred of my sinning soul."

He flicks open the front clasp of my bra, fingertips skimming my breasts as he removes it from me completely. Then he slides my panties down my legs until I'm completely exposed—bare, trembling and so much in love with this tortured man whom I will betray to protect. But not now. Not here. Until we leave this place, he is mine to care for.

"God can decide what to do with my body and soul once it is his to govern. But today I give myself to you. My angel. My love. My Evangeline."

My breath catches as he removes his own shirt, his pants and what he wears beneath. All that is left is a gold chain with a cross dangling like a pendulum above me.

"Benedict," I start, but I don't have the right words to say to this beautiful man who has given up everything, who is giving himself over to me. As much as my heart cries out for him, my body responds by welcoming him, my clit swelling between my legs, causing me to writhe against the sheets.

"You were my first client," I blurt, needing him to know that I did what I did out of necessity. That I was never practiced in this art.

"And there will be no more," he says, his voice laced with a type of possession I wish would last a lifetime. "But I'm afraid I don't have— I was not anticipating—"

I let out a bittersweet laugh. "I am protected," I say, understanding his worry. "I have to be. In case anyone…" But I don't want to think about being with anyone in this way but him. I don't want to dwell on what might have been if I was not sent to Benedict first.

I reach for his cock, my thumb swirling the precum over his tip, and then I pull it toward my opening, letting out a soft moan as he rubs against me. I'm already slick between my folds, ready to take him in.

"Are you sure?" I ask. "This is what you want?"

Without another word, he sinks inside me to the very hilt, a primal growl tearing from his lips, and I arch against him as I cry out his name.

"Christ," he says through gritted teeth, but his word is not meant for prayer.

And he does not ask for forgiveness.

CHAPTER SIXTEEN

Benedict

MY WORLD IS EVANGELINE, and Evangeline is my
world. I hold still and absorb the magnitude of this
moment, savor the fact that I am inside a woman—
and not just any woman, but one whom I love. It is
not just the eight inches of my body inserted into her
wet, tight heat like a well-fitting glove, but it is our
very souls connecting. There is no she or me, just a
communion of sweat, salt, love and desire.

"Please," she begs, making near-inarticulate purrs.
"Please."

What we share is as old as the stone surrounding
us, an ancient dance that my body understands, despite the fact this is my first time. I roll my hips, unable to bear exiting completely, and then rock back
in.

As much as I want to look at her face until her
image is seared into my mind like a permanent tattoo, I close my eyes, needing to feel her more. Every
sweet square inch of her silken folds and satiny tunnel. No fabrics at the finest dress shops in Paris,

New York or London can compare with the exquisite softness of my Evangeline's gorgeous pussy.

She lifts her hips to meet my next thrust, and my thick shaft traces over her hardening pearl-like center. At the same time, her inner muscles clench my cock, milking me hard. Fuck. She blows my mind.

"Do that again," she murmurs.

"Oh yeah. Again and again," I rumble. This time I clench my ass and put more force into my glide, ensuring her swollen clit gets every inch of my royal treatment. The slapping sound fills the cave, our lovemaking hot and raw. This isn't mindless fucking, but savage joining, bittersweet because it cannot be forever.

But it is now.

And it must be enough.

She wraps her thighs around my hips, her heels finding grip against my ass, and I know that I am lying.

This will never be enough.

This is what I was born to do.

Desperation explodes within me. It's like I'm in a candy store and have been told I can have anything I want, but only for the next ten minutes. My mouth fastens on the peak of her nipple, and I suck, then let my lower teeth graze the pale skin, and she arches against me. As I turn to give my attention to the other, I lower my hand, grasping her ass while I roll over, letting her be on top.

I remain in a half-sit, laving her nipples while she rides me buck wild. It's all I can do to hang on to her undulating body. The scruff from my five-o'clock shadow skims her wet, flushed flesh. She leans into me with a cry, and my fingers slide into the cleft of her backside. I skim her tight rosebud, not entering, but keeping up a light pressure as I enjoy the show.

She raises her arms up over her head, twining her long hair through her fingers, luxuriating in the feel of me filling her with everything I have to give. I use my other hand to thrum her clit in relentless circles that echo the rhythm of her hips.

She's so wet and I shove her backward, mouth-watering, needing a taste of that sweet pussy. I'm rough, but no less rough than she, as I part her folds with my thumbs and drag my tongue over her tangy slit, her nails biting into my shoulders.

"God. Benedict. Oh my God, yes, right there."

I drink her like she is a sacrament, like she is salvation, and every lick is heaven.

"Inside me," she begs. "I want you to feel me come for you."

She doesn't have to ask twice. I throw her on her stomach, burying myself back inside. Her ass nestles again my abs. I brace myself with one hand and use the other to skim over her beautiful bouncing breasts, the concave dip of her belly, the flare to her hip, and I nestle at the apex of her need.

I can go deeper in the position, but what I don't count on is how much deeper I can go into myself. I am discovering a wellspring of powerful love and tenderness that I never knew I was capable of feeling. My entire body feels like nothing more than a vessel to worship this woman until the end of time.

But we don't have that long, and I need to make every second count. I bend and run the underside of my lower lip between her shoulder blades. I breathe in her scent. There is so much that I need to tell her, but I am not sure if I have the words. So I turn to the vocabulary of gentle kisses and teasing clitoral swirls.

"Come with me," she urges, her voice cracking with urgency. "Now."

Evangeline

Benedict stills inside me and pulls out, and for a second I wonder if he's already regretting this, stopping before we can finish.

"I need to see you, angel," he says in a hoarse whisper. "I need to look into your eyes when we take this leap together."

I roll over, any physical pain I might have felt now nothing more than a distant ache, and there he is, towering over me with such love in his eyes I wonder how I'll ever survive the fallout of what I must do tonight.

I stroke a finger over the cut on his thigh, telling myself that the wound is only superficial. But how deep will the hurt go when I break his trust?

"Benedict," I say, my voice cracking, and I think I might tell him everything.

But he reaches toward my face, his thumb brushing away a tear when I hadn't even realized I was crying.

"Let me take the pain away, Evangeline."

Then he bends over to kiss me, his lips sweet and featherlight against mine before he fills me anew. I cannot stop the tears as he thrusts inside me, again and again, his eyes locked on mine.

"I love you," he says. "Always."

Then he plunges deeper than I knew any man could go, filling not only my body, but my entire heart and soul.

"Always, Benedict." He presses a hand between us, his thumb on my clit, and I buck against him, insatiable. Our short time together can never be enough.

Together we fly off the edge in undeniable ecstasy, a savage growl tearing from Benedict's lips as I cry out his name.

He collapses next to me, chest heaving as he cradles me in his arms. He kisses me, and I taste the salt of tears, not sure if they are his or mine—or maybe both.

"I didn't know it could be like this," he whispers, and all I can do is nod, to speak to him only through lips touching lips, or else I will crumble to a million pieces, my heart trampled to dust.

Hours later, we sit in a helicopter, piloted by X, as he tells us what should be good news. Camille and Lola have been reunited and are hidden in a village until it is safe for them to return. But my chest is heavy with the weight of what's to come—of what I still stand to lose.

"Also," he says into his headset microphone, "I did not want to mention it this morning." He raises a brow. "I felt the whole breaking your brother's wife out of prison situation was enough to focus on."

"What is it?" Benedict asks, squeezing my hand.

My mind wanders, wishing we were far away from here. "I've deciphered the map."

X's voice comes through loud and clear in my own headset, but his words do not register.

"What?" I ask, my eyes widening.

Benedict leans forward toward the cockpit. "Where does it lead?"

X holds up a hand, signaling for the prince to wait, and my stomach feels as if it has leaped to my throat. Maybe this will be good news—something that will mean I won't have to betray my family or the man I love.

We're landing.

Minutes later we touch down on the royal helipad, and we wait several minutes for X to power down the beast and for the propellers to stop.

X exits the aircraft, and then Benedict follows so the two of them can help me to the ground. I limp to a waiting vehicle, a BMW SUV.

"Ah," Benedict says. "Damien's car that he left behind. Father gave this to him before he was even old enough to drive it—legally. Now, from what I know, he only drives the sleekest of racing automobiles. And he's quite good, I hear."

Benedict says his banished brother's name in a wistful tone, and I realize there is so much of this man's history I do not know.

"We should at least get you to the palace doctor," he says as I wince lowering myself into the car.

I shake my head. "I want to know what the map says. I want to see what my father and brother were hiding."

X pulls his door closed in front and turns to face us.

"What we were hiding," he says. "I know Jasper

Vernazza well. And I think it's time I tell you everything, Miss Evangeline."

Benedict gets his wish—as do I. We sit in his private library, X laying out the map on a table before
us as the palace doctor does his best to examine me.

"It seems to be a nasty sprain," the man says as he
props my foot on a pillow and places a cooling pack
on my knee. "You should stay off it for a few days."

Benedict stands above me, arms crossed. "I'll see
to it, Doctor."

"But this gash on your cheek..." he adds. "Are
you sure you merely scratched it? The bruising says
otherwise."

Benedict's eyes darken. "What do you mean?"

The doctor strokes a short, dark beard. "The se-
verity of the bruise and the swiftness with which it
has appeared speaks to blunt trauma."

"I think I might have bumped it on my fall, as
well," I blurt, remembering the force of that woman's
hand against my face. It takes all of my will to keep
myself from shaking, to convince everyone that what
I speak is the truth.

The doctor lets out a sigh. "I do recommend X-rays
for both injuries. The fact that you can limp suggests
a sprain, but the swelling can be hiding something we
can't see. And that bruise?" He shakes his head. "I'd
hate for there to be a chipped bone in that beautiful
face. Promise me that you will get to the hospital in
the next day or so after you've rested."

I nod, seemingly appeasing all three men, and the
doctor bows to the prince before taking his leave.

Benedict sits on the couch beside me, softly stroking my battered cheek with the tips of his fingers.

"Is there anything you're not telling me?" he asks.

I swallow the lump in my throat and shake my head.

"I jumped off a moving train," I say. "I think that's enough to do a girl in."

And watching my brother almost get beaten to death.

He kisses me softly. "Of course, angel."

I let out a breath. "X," I say. "Tell me everything."

CHAPTER SEVENTEEN

Benedict

"Everything?" X arches a brow after showing the doctor out and locking the door behind him. He then heads to the windows and pulls the blinds, even though we are on an upper floor in the tower library. His shoulders heave in an inward sigh. "Very well. Why don't we start here?" He blows across the map. Dust motes fly off the parchment, filtering through the lamp-lit air.

I rub my hand over my thigh, trying to subtly knead out the muscle tension. Of course there is a bad feeling welling inside me. Only hours ago I buried my shaft in the silken cleft of the woman beside me, this amazing and devoted sister and aunt who is going to stop at nothing to reunite her brother with his wife and child.

"Where is *here*?" Evangeline asks, oh-so-naturally lacing her fingers with mine. She has no idea that she destroys me with the gentle caress.

"At the start of all good stories." X jabs a finger in the top left corner of the map. "The beginning of everything."

Beginning.

The word seeps into my skin like vitriolic acid. We sit and discuss beginnings when too soon my time with Evangeline will come to an end. Perhaps this is my great spiritual test, to be confronted by my heart's desire, be offered it freely and without equivocation. But I must lead myself not into temptation and instead deliver myself from evil.

Except there isn't an evil bone in Evangeline. She is an angel in female form. Good to her core. Why can't I have her? Why can't I walk a different path than the one paved for me by expectation and family tradition?

I know the answer, and it lies deeper than a boy so desperate for his father's attention. The sins of the mother. That is what I must contend with. So much has gone wrong in our family and it's up to me to do my part to put things to right.

I grip her hand tighter than intended, and she is alarmed.

"Benedict…are you all right?"

"Sorry, angel," I mutter. "Please proceed, X."

"I have to make a confession. When we discovered the map behind the angel, I was not entirely truthful on a few matters." He meets my gaze and holds it steadily. "Allow me to rectify. This forest stretches from beyond the palace walls to the peaks that separate Edenvale from Nightgardin." X waves a hand over a dark shadowed area on the map. "Here is where our story begins. The Tale of The Order."

"Let me guess," Evangeline says in a teasing tone. "You're one of them, a covert secret soldier charged with guarding and protecting Edenvale."

"Do not laugh," X orders. "This isn't a game. Our neighbors to the north want something very badly. The Spring of Youth."

I blink. "How do you know if the old story is real? Have you ever seen the Spring?"

"Highness." X regards me a long time. "Recall the story of Doubting Thomas? He doubted the risen Christ until he was able to touch the wounds with his hands, look upon the Lord's face with his own two eyes."

"Of course I do," I say testily. "But what you ask me to believe is…is…"

"A matter of faith," Evangeline breathes.

X nods. "Exactly. There are things at work around us that most never see, nor need to understand. The Order prefers it that way. No member since the original cohort who made the map have ever set eyes on it. Better to keep away."

"Lead us not into temptation," I murmur.

"So let me get this straight. The Order protects… access to the *actual* Spring of Youth?" Evangeline says slowly.

"Yes," X replies. "Among other things."

She knits her brows. "And my brother and father were members?"

X nods. "Who performed their assigned duties with distinction and valor. They embody the very spirit that makes The Order the last line of defense against evil temptation in the world. Nine hundred years ago King Randall the Fair discovered the Spring. He was consumed by beauty and youth even as the waters began to corrode his mind. Eventually his brother, King Humbert the Just, overthrew him in a coup. And it is from Humbert that the Lorentz line descends. Disgraced, Randall moved to Nightgardin, where in his addled state he revealed the secrets of the Spring. Nightgardin began making incursions into our realm to find it and The Order was subsequently formed by King Humbert to seal the Spring forever and defend it against those who wish to exploit its power. After all, aging is as much a part of life as is youth, and beauty is more than skin-deep."

I swing my gaze to X. "You know a great deal about The Order."

"Like I said, I wasn't entirely truthful in your library the night we discovered the map." X closes his eyes a moment before removing his suit jacket and placing it neatly on the closest chair. "I couldn't tell you about my membership without securing permission from our leader." Then he rolls up his shirtsleeve and there, on his bicep, over the defined ridge of flexed muscle, is a tattooed crow's feather.

Evangeline

I hold in my surprise. "Jasper and my father always maintained the crow tattoo was a Vernazza family symbol. I never questioned it as all the men in my family bore the mark."

X nods. "Some women as well, but never both spouses. Dedication to The Order is an honor and a privilege—but the dangers are also quite great. To allow a husband and a wife to serve together—"

"Could mean leaving your children orphans," I interrupt as my throat feels like it's closing in. "Yet here I am an orphan anyway. My brother and his family are all I have."

Benedict pulls me to him and buries his face in my hair. "I'm so sorry, angel. We will get your brother back. I'm not sure how, but it will happen."

I let out a shaky breath against his strong chest. I know how to get him back. By betraying that which Jasper almost gave his life to protect.

"Members are gathering," X says. "I assure you we will bring him to safety. And we will ensure the Spring's protection, as well."

I pull away from Benedict and nod. "I'm tired," I lie, trying to keep my voice steady. "I think I'd like to lie down."

X bows his head. "Of course. This is a lot to take in. There is more to show you about the map, but it can wait for now. We will make our move when the nearest members of my brethren arrive. It will not be long."

Benedict helps me out of the library and up the spiral staircase to his apartment.

"Too much has been thrown at you today," he says as we make our way to his bedroom. "I will leave you to rest while X and I figure out what's next."

"Stay with me?" I ask, voice trembling now. It is too early to say goodbye, and I need to take my fill of him before I leave.

I sit on the edge of the bed, and he settles next to me.

"Anything, angel. Anything you need."

I can hear a similar sorrow in his own words, one that says he knows we will be parted all too soon.

But he believes we have weeks left, while I know this night will be our last.

"Make love to me," I say, a simple plea, and he does not hesitate before kissing me.

His lips are soft and gentle, as if he understands we need to savor this experience. He undresses me, his movements slow and deliberate, kissing every inch of my skin as he bares my body to his loving gaze.

He lays me on my back and runs a finger from my chest to my stomach, and then down between my legs, entering me with one soft glide.

"I could touch you like this every minute of every hour of the day," he says, his voice rough as gravel.

"And I would let you," I tell him, my words barely heard. He slips another finger inside me and dips between my bent knees. His tongue is warm as it expertly swirls around my swollen center, like he's done this a hundred times. But my body is the only one he's ever truly known, and it is as if he was born to touch me like this.

I let out a whimper, and Benedict responds with a savage groan.

"To taste you," he says, peering up to look at me, "is second only to breathing."

His fingers pump inside me, and I arch. My fingers curl into his sheets, but I feel like I cannot get any purchase. He will send me over the edge in mere seconds, and I am powerless to stop him.

"Benedict," I cry. "I don't want to do this alone."

He pulls his hand free, only long enough to remove his own clothing. And then without another word, he sinks into me, and my heart threatens to explode.

I wrap my arms around his neck and pull his lips to mine, the taste of him and of me mingled as one.

Deep as he is, every inch buried to the hilt, it's like I cannot get enough.

"More, Benedict," I say. "I need more."

He lifts his head and then dips it toward my breasts, where he licks and nips at my sensitive peaks, all the while pounding himself straight through to my core. I arch into him, raking my fingernails down his no-longer-welted back, though I'm sure I now draw blood.

A thunderous roar rips from his chest as his arms snake under my back. He lifts me to him, our bodies slick with sweat, and I truly do not know where I end and he begins.

"Come for me, angel," he says against my lips, and then his hand slides to the place where we're joined, his thumb against my swollen clit, and he takes me to the brink and straight over the edge with him.

Tears stream as wave after wave of ecstasy takes over me.

We collapse onto the bed, Benedict still inside me, as my muscles contract around him.

"I love you," I say as we lie there entwined, our limbs exquisitely tangled.

"And I will never know love such as this again," he says. "You are my world, Evangeline. I would trade my soul not to leave you—if I could."

And I would give my life for him—for all those I love. And soon that is exactly what I will do.

I'm not sure how long we stay that way, but eventually Benedict nods off, and I am forced to leave the love of my life.

* * *

When I have dressed and put myself together as best I can, he is still in the deepest of sleep. So I kiss his forehead—one final connection—grabbing the supplies I need and taking my leave.

In the library I do what is necessary before I roll up the map and tuck it under my arm. Then I do the best to explain myself, to pray that the man who nearly gave his soul to love me will someday also grant me forgiveness. Someday—when I can tell him everything. But I have to save his and Jasper's lives first.

> My Dearest Benedict,
> Please know that I have no choice. The last thing I want to do is betray your trust, but this is the only way to save the one other person I love most—my brother. They will kill him if I don't deliver the map. They may kill him anyway, and me, but at least I'll know I tried. And I'll know that you are safe from this mess I've dragged you into. Be sure of one thing, though. I love you to the depths of my soul. Whether my time on this earth ends tonight or several years from now, it will be you who lives within my heart until the very end.
> I love you. Always.
> Evangeline

It takes me nearly thirty minutes to limp to the cottage in my condition, but I make it just before midnight. When I enter, I see my time with Benedict in flashes of scenery—trying on beautiful dresses, teasing him at the game table, watching him watch me in the bedroom.

I sit in my chair at the game table, imagining Benedict sitting across from me. I reach underneath, feeling for what I know is there, the one pullout compartment that was empty of game pieces. In it I leave my gift to Benedict. Then I retreat to my bedroom and wait.

My body convulses with a shudder. This man trusted me with everything, and I have kept him in the dark when I need him most. At least he has X and The Order to keep him safe.

X.

The Madam couldn't possibly know about X being a member. There's no way she would have let me stay here if she knew I was under the protection of The Order. She threatened Benedict's safety if I told him what was happening tonight. But maybe he and X can help.

I sit on the bed and pull out my phone. For so long I've felt the burden of protecting those I love. Perhaps it's time I lean on someone else for a change.

I dial the number X gave me in case of emergency, but just as I hit Send, the floorboard creaks behind me.

I gasp as an arm snakes around my waist, then drop the phone when a hand covers my mouth.

"No time for second thoughts, dearie," a gruff female voice says. "Looks like we can't trust you to keep quiet after all."

I don't have a chance to protest as she drags me and the map toward the trapdoor. I scrape my hand against the floor, snagging my phone and shoving it in my pocket before we slip down, down, down below the surface.

When we reach solid ground, she throws me to the dirt floor, my head landing at a steel-toed boot. I look up to see the Madam, dressed in all black, a thief who blends into the night. All that lights my vision is a torch she holds in her right hand.

She nudges my injured knee with her boot, then presses her toe into it until I cry out.

"Welcome to the catacombs," she says. "Now let's go find us a magic spring."

CHAPTER EIGHTEEN

Benedict

MY ENTIRE BODY is slick with sweat. A nightmare. I've had a nightmare. One where Evangeline was lost in the dark, afraid, in danger, and no matter how hard I tried, I couldn't find her. I roll over to gather her close, steady myself with the rhythm of her breath. But her spot in the bed is empty. My stomach muscles contract in time with my jaw. The sheets are cool as well as the goose-down pillow, no lingering trace of body heat. She's been gone for some time. I sit and rake a hand through my hair.

"Angel?"

No soft, lilting voice answers.

I rise from my bed, tug on my black boxer briefs, a pair of gray sweats and a white T-shirt. The clock reads just after midnight. Where are you, Evangeline? I walk through my apartment and find no sign of her. I freeze as I open the door and gaze at the staircase.

The library. The map.

Hairs bristle on my nape. Every step down to the second floor heightens the strange, foreboding sensation in my soul. When I enter the library, it is empty. A faint smell of perfume wafts through the air beneath the dusty scent of ancient books. Slowly, as if caught by a magnetic force, my gaze swings to a small envelope on the center table.

Benedict. My name is written in a small neat script.

I bite on the inside of my cheek, a metallic taste flooding my mouth as I take the envelope in hand. Letters left in the dark of night seldom contain good news.

I read her hastily written farewell, and her betrayal. The words lance me like a hundred knives. Joy can fill the deepest caverns of one's heart and soul, but that is also how great the sorrow is when that joy is gone.

I am alone in an abyss. Forsaken by love.

She has left and taken the map to make a devil's bargain.

"No!" I sweep my hand across the closest shelf. Glass baubles and trinkets fly to the floor and shatter into a million pieces, impossible to put back together, just like my heart. "No."

Metal grinds and creaks behind me. I whirl around to see one of the bookcases swing open. X emerges from the shadows dressed head to toe in black tactical gear.

"Angel…" It is all I can say.

Evangeline has betrayed me, X, this kingdom. But I cannot bring myself to hate her for a decision made out of love for her brother, her only living family.

"I will go into the catacombs to get her. Alone," X says. "She has her phone with her." He lifts his own and the Find My Phone app shows a small dot on the move.

"The fuck you will," I growl. "As if I'd allow you to leave me behind."

"I know you want answers as to her choices." He shoves a hand in his pocket. "I also know you wouldn't want to see her hurt, or worse, but remember. You're determined to enter the priesthood. This is a way to let me get Evangeline out of your life—safely, of course. Once gone, she will tempt you no more."

My whole body stills. X offers me two distinct paths for the rest of my life. If I take the former, then I will not let my father down. I will be the good bastard who atones for the sins of the mother. I will be the dutiful second son who doesn't rock the boat. Who accepts the destiny mapped out for me. If I let him seek Evangeline alone, I will be able to consecrate my life to good works. No one will know what happened. How I gave my heart—and so much more—realizing what can take place between a man and a woman is more than mere lust, but a holy act of union.

But it all feels like a choice offered to another. Not me.

Because it isn't a choice at all.

You can't choose to breathe. Or have your heart beat. And that's how loving Evangeline feels to me. It is a basic, primal part of who I am. And if she has truly betrayed me, I need to hear her explanation with my gaze fastened on her face.

"Let's go. We don't have a second to lose."

X nods. "Follow me." He leads me out of the tower

and across the grounds, through the maze to the gardener's cottage. There are signs of struggle in the bedroom, fingernail marks on the old wooden floor. Rage rises within me, red-hot. When I get to the people who took Evangeline, they will see no mercy from me. I will be an avenging angel raining fire and brimstone. Even if she stole from and lied to me, I can't cut off my feelings.

The door in the floor is still open, and we enter the catacombs, trading the world of the living for that of the dead.

X lights a torch I didn't know he had with him, but then again he never ceases to surprise me. The air down here is strange, dense. Our footsteps make no echo. We occasionally have to duck and weave around thick roots, and every once in a while there is a sound of dripping water or a rodent scurrying from our approach.

I try not to look upon the walls, lined with skulls, the hollow eyes and gaping teeth seeming to mock my intentions.

We reach a T-junction.

"Left or right?" I mutter.

X checks his phone. "Right."

I turn to go when something stills my step.

"Your mother's tomb," X says in a reverential tone.

A weight presses on my chest as I stare at the marble-faced statue of a woman in front of a large sarcophagus covered in fresh flowers. The crypt is candlelit but cold, a lonely place to spend eternity.

"What kind of man would she have wanted me to be?" I ask, my throat tight.

X regards me with eyes that are twin pools of black ink. I cannot read what is written there.

"One who was happy," he says curtly.

Then a memory slams me with the force of a bullet. A kiss on the forehead in the middle of the night. A whisper in my ear, a voice I haven't heard in over two decades but know to my bones is that of my mother.

Be brave in the days ahead. And above all else in your life, find joy—and do good. You can have everything if you choose wisely.

My eyes burn as I stare at her statue. She said I had a choice. But the choice ahead? My joy lies not in consecrating life to God. It is to live to the end of my days beside the woman I seek. To her I shall consecrate everything, my days, my life, my soul.

Perhaps I've known this for some time, even if I couldn't fully articulate the thought. My heart pounds. "How can I abandon the woman that I... *love* for the church? It's an impossible choice for me to make. I might let down the king, but I would be honoring the wishes of my queen, and in that I find strength."

"Your mother loved you very much, Benedict. More than you can possibly imagine."

I want to ask more, ask how he knows, but now is not the time.

We set off again, this time in a dead run. Sweat slicks my back, my T-shirt clinging to my skin. Each gasp shreds my lungs. I lose track of the minutes as my legs pump in a sprint. How long have we been here? Five minutes? Five hours?

Then in the distance, I hear a sound that isn't water or rats. A sound that turns my veins to ice.

Evangeline's scream.

Evangeline

I taste blood, coppery and warm, before I spit and see crimson spray across the stone floor of some chamber they've dragged me to beneath the palace grounds.

"You already know what the map says," I growl. "Otherwise we wouldn't be here."

She clucks her tongue. "Ah, ah, ah, my dear Evangeline," she lilts. "You're holding out on me. What I seek is down here. Yes. But only the map's hidden text can tell us exactly where." She nods to a slab of rock where the map is laid out for her to study. "You've found what I seek—you and your precious prince. Surely you've deciphered it, as well."

I'm hauled to my feet now by my old friend the warden while the Madam says, "Again, Gideon."

Gideon, the third member of our party, is the soldier with the strawberry birthmark on his cheek who'd been assigned to guard my cottage in the maze. If I had to guess his age from his eyes, I'd say he'd lived several lifetimes, and none of them good. But his features are that of a young man, possibly even younger than me.

His lips curl into a sneer before his stony hand makes contact with my face once more. I shriek as my head snaps back, and I see stars. And though I stumble, ready to welcome hard, unforgiving ground, my captor doesn't let me fall. Instead, she pulls me tight against her as my knees buckle, forcing me to stare straight ahead with an eye that is quickly swelling shut—into Gideon's lifeless gaze.

"Perhaps that jogged your memory?" the Madam says with the demeanor of one enjoying her afternoon tea.

She steps forward, an ominous laugh dribbling off her lips. She swipes a thumb under my swollen eye, and I draw in a sharp breath. Her skin comes away slick with my blood. She stares at it before wiping it clean on her black pants.

"Young, vital blood runs in those veins of yours. And soon, when I taste the eternal water, it will run through mine. Only then will I be able to dispose of you. But first I have to tell you the good news. It seems that Jasper—despite his severe and life-threatening injuries—has taken to talking in his sleep. And hell if he isn't trying to tell us what we need to know now that it's almost too late." She hums. "By the light of the moon, Evangeline. Remember. By the light of the moon."

The words might as well be another language. All I ever knew of my brother was his quiet nature, his love of art. This Jasper she speaks of is a stranger to me. But he is still alive. It is this thought alone that keeps me from going under. I can still save him. Somehow. Even if it means lying through my teeth to do it. All I need is to buy myself time and hope that my call to X went through, that he knows I'm in trouble.

I try to feign a look of realization but doubt anything can be read from my expression other than pain and fear.

"You know what he speaks of. Do you not?" the Madam asks.

I nod.

"And yet you would have me believe otherwise?" She leans close enough that I feel her on my skin. "Evangeline—it seems you need to be punished."

She nods toward the woman who holds me upright, and in a flash I'm on the ground, the heel of the brutish woman's boot pressing into my knee. Something cracks, and I scream, the pain white-hot as it shoots through me.

But then the pressure is gone, and I hear the sickening sound of flesh being pierced before the woman who was towering over me pitches toward the ground. I have to roll out of the way to avoid being crushed.

My vision clears to show her lying beside me with a dagger protruding from her chest.

The Madam hisses, and she jumps in front of Gideon, her eyes darting from left to right.

"Come out, come out, wherever you are," she singsongs, but there is a heightened edge to her tone. "Surely you know I have your angel," she says. "If you want me not to finish her off, you'll be smart and show yourself."

I try to scramble backward, but the pain in my leg is too great.

That's when I see him. As if born from the darkness, Benedict emerges, haloed in a pool of light.

I'm dead, I think. I'm dead, and my prince—my love—has come to welcome me into whatever afterlife will have me. This can't be heaven. I don't deserve it. The sight of the man I betrayed must have been sent to torment me.

"Release her," Benedict says. "You have committed enough crimes against Edenvale. I'm sure you don't want to add another murder to the list."

He speaks so calmly and of such things as sparing me that I almost believe he might be here to rescue me.

The Madam cackles and steps aside, revealing Gideon.

"No," I croak. If Benedict really is here, I will not watch him perish, too. "No!" I cry louder, pushing myself up to my elbow.

My prince's eyes find mine, and I watch the color drain from his face. His jaw clenches.

"You," he says to Gideon. "You did that to her?" He moves to strike, but not before his gaze falls on me again. This is all it takes to give Gideon his opening, and he delivers a swift kick to Benedict's ribs.

He grunts and stumbles, but he does not fall. Instead, he straightens, his face split into a knowing grin.

"You're going to have to do better than that, boy," Benedict says. "Because I'm not leaving here without Evangeline—without making you pay for hurting her and betraying your sworn duty as a royal guard."

Gideon strikes with his fist this time, but Benedict ducks the blow, taking Gideon by surprise as he punches him in the face. Gideon's head swings to the side, and I see crimson streaming from his nose.

He laughs, his tongue lapping at the liquid as it flows over his lips. The Madam crosses her arms and grins at the display before her.

Gideon strikes again, this time catching Benedict in the jaw, and I yelp as I see a spray of blood fly from his mouth. But he still doesn't fall, this time sweeping his leg across Gideon's, the boy falling to his back.

Benedict sneers at him, but Gideon rises with lightning-quick speed, as if he thrives on the pain. Because despite his bloodied face from what must be a broken nose, he acts as if it is nothing more than a scratch.

After one of Gideon's blows, Benedict calls out. "A little help now, X?"

And out of the shadows walks the prince's guard, twirling another dagger in his hand.

Gideon freezes, as does the Madam.

"I thought you were doing quite well. But if you require assistance, I am, of course, at your service."

X points the knife at the Madam, and she takes a step away. Then he points it at Gideon.

"No!" she yelps.

Benedict shakes out his hand, his knuckles bloodied. X nods toward the stone slab and the map.

"Your choice," X says. "You can leave with the map or with your progeny."

Progeny? Gideon is the Madam's son? But how? She couldn't be more than a decade older than me.

"Look at me," the Madam says, a certain desperation in her tone. "Do you know how many procedures, how many injections it takes to keep myself looking like this? I was the most beautiful woman in The Jewel Box, but now I'm surpassed by all those girls with their youth and dewy skin. I've had enough of doctors and needles. Nightgardin came to me last year. They

made me a promise. Deliver the map—deciphered—
and I'd get to drink from the waters. No more going
under the knife!"

"Not tonight, you're not," Benedict says with quiet
confidence.

The Madam's lips curl into a wicked grin. "She
will never be safe. Your precious Evangeline." She
spares me a glance. "Not as long as we still seek the
Spring and she holds the answer."

X strolls toward Gideon, touching the pointed
steel of the dagger to the boy's chest. He traces a
small circle over his heart, and the Madam takes a
deep breath.

X pulls up his sleeve to reveal the mark of The
Order. Behind him, several more men and a few
women—all dressed in black from head to toe—
step forward, as well.

"As long as we are here," X says, "and we will
always be here, Nightgardin will not harm the children of Vernazza again—or any member of the royal
family. If so, we will seek retribution, and I do not
think your benefactors want a war. You've lost. Accept what is true. The location of the Spring will
never fall into Nightgardin possession."

The Madam reaches for Gideon's hand and tugs
him to her side.

"We are not through, X," she hisses, then turns
toward a passageway I had not seen before.

"I'm through with you," I say, then despite the pain
that rips through every muscle, through the bones in
my leg I know are broken, I launch myself forward
and grab the Madam by the ankle. She pitches forward, landing face-first on the stony ground.

A guttural roar rips from her chest as she scrambles to her feet, blood streaming from her now misshapen nose.

"I'll kill you!" she cries, lunging for me, but she is intercepted by one of the hooded women of The Order. Gideon is subdued by one of the men.

"It's fake," I say, knowing this woman will kill me if she ever gets the chance, but I need Benedict to know. "The map is fake. I painted a replica and hid the original." My eyes meet Benedict's. "I needed you to believe the betrayal so you'd be safe. She said they'd kill you if…"

The last of my adrenaline seeps from my pores, but before I slump to the ground, Benedict is there. He scoops me into his arms, and tears stream from my eyes when I see his bruised and battered face.

"You came for me," I say, my voice trembling. "After what I did, you came."

He nods. "And I almost lost you," he says through gritted teeth. "Evangeline—" But he stops himself, his voice cracking on my name.

The Madam—shouting furiously—and Gideon are dragged away, hopefully where they can never harm my family again.

"We need to get her to the hospital at once," X says. "I've just received word that Jasper is there, too. My brethren will stand guard at his door. No one else is to be trusted now."

"Of course," Benedict says, pulling me closer to him. He opens his mouth to say something more, but no words come.

"We got here in time," X says to him. "That is what matters."

Pain courses through my bones, through every nerve ending, but I wrap my arms around Benedict's neck, afraid if I don't I will lose him forever.

"The game table," I whisper into his ear. "I hid it beneath the game table. Please forgive me."

Then darkness pulls me under.

CHAPTER NINETEEN

Benedict

THE DOCTORS SAY she should have regained consciousness by now. They come by on their rounds and examine her with furrowed brows. I dislike their thoughtful, pensive frowning. Once, not so long ago, I, too, was a man of pondering, of reticence. Now the time for measured thinking seems too slow.

I am not the person that I once was.

I want action. Fuck it. I want *them* to take action, and bring her back. But the choice to wake is hers and hers alone.

"Evangeline, angel, please. Open your beautiful eyes," I urge her. "I have so much to tell you, my love. So many things are now in perspective."

"Love?" a deep voice says from the hospital room doorway. "What the hell is going on here, son?"

I glance up to see a man standing there, watching me with a stunned expression etched into the weathered lines of his face.

"Father," I say. What is he doing here?

"X rang me," he says, answering my thoughts.

He steps forward, posture perfectly erect. "I say,

it was presumptuous for a bodyguard to use my personal phone line, but he seems to think that you and I have some talking to do. I didn't know what he meant, except now I can see. While I've been busy handling Edenvale diplomacy at the United Nations, you've been busy with a whore." He snorts. "I was skeptical about your older brother choosing his matchmaker, but at least she made an honest living. This woman… Son, you employed her to tempt you from the cloth, and she has succeeded. Why should I rejoice?"

I cross the room in a flash. "That woman you are so quick to disparage almost died to protect me—to protect Edenvale. Tread carefully here, Father. Because if you call her a whore one more time, I will make sure it's the last word you ever utter."

The two hulking men who stand at a short distance behind the king make menacing sounds deep in their tattooed throats. I ignore their little alpha charade with a sneer. If they want to bark, then I'll show that I have bite.

"Evangeline is not a whore," I say. "And even if she were, it is of no matter, for I have given her my heart forever and more."

Father's mouth opens and closes. "Impossible."

"I am not going to join the priesthood." The words aren't as difficult to speak as I feared. In fact, they feel like the most natural thing I have said to him since I can remember. "You will have to punish me in a different way."

His brows raise. "Punish?" He crosses his arms in a gesture that makes him look, for the barest second, exactly like our missing youngest brother.

"For being the bastard," I snarl. "For being the living embodiment of mother's shame. But all she wanted for me was happiness. And making the woman I love the happiest woman on God's earth is my new mission in life. If you knew what she did for our kingdom's protection—"

"Bastard?" Father retreats a step. "You can't mean to say you believe those discredited old rumors. We never were sure of the source, but they seemed to have been started by our enemies in Nightgardin."

Rumors? All my life I'd grown up with whispers. Worse yet, I heard no one deny them. So yes. I believed in the stain that I thought I bore, in my responsibility to cleanse it.

"I am truly your son?" The impact of his words hits me with unexpected force. I physically brace myself with the door frame.

He inclines his head, a look of shame crossing his face. "If you ever heard lies and believed them, the fault is my own. I'll admit I once had a brief moment of doubt, to the point where I requested a paternity test from the doctor who delivered you. It was the only serious fight your mother and I ever had. The tests showed that you were my son, and I spent the rest of our short marriage trying to make up for my lack of faith in her loyalty and love."

"But I look the least like you," I murmur.

"Yes," he agrees. "You are your own person. But if you are willing to fight for the woman you love, I can see that we have something in common." He clasps me on the shoulder. "I won't deny that family tradition is important to me, as is my faith. To have you become a priest would have filled me with great pride. But I also want you to choose the path that is right for you, my son."

Pounding feet echo up the corridor. There is shouting. My brother Nikolai bursts around the corridor, his new bride, Kate, hot on his heels.

"Jesus, Benedict." He pulls up short. His skin is tanned a golden brown from their Hawaiian vacation. "X sent a Learjet for us and a dossier bringing me up to speed." He looks over my shoulder. "We go on a short island vacation and the whole palace goes to hell. Is that her? The woman?"

"The woman I love," I correct. "The woman I hope to make my wife."

"Benedict?"

My throat tightens as I slowly turn around.

Evangeline's lids flutter. Her pupils are dilated, but her gaze is strong and intense.

"Angel—you're awake."

Evangeline

I try to sit, but everything in me screams in pain. I shudder, and Benedict is at my bedside before I can exhale.

"You need more morphine," he says. "I'll call a nurse. I...I need to let the doctors know—"

I use what little strength I have to rest a reassuring hand on his—a hand now adorned with medical tape, an IV and a pulse monitor on my finger.

"No medicine yet," I say, my swollen lip making it hard to speak. "I want to think clearly. Are we... Are we safe?" I ask, the events of the late-night hours coming back with unforgiving force. The pulse monitor starts beeping, and Benedict leans over to smooth my hair.

"You're safe, angel. They cannot hurt you again. I promise you that."

"And Jasper? Did you find Jasper?"

He nods. "He is not conscious yet, but members of The Order stand guard outside his room, and the doctors say his body is healing. You both are under The Order's protection for the entirety of your existence. You will not be harmed again."

His voice catches, and I run a thumb over the bruises and small cuts that pepper his face. He leans into it, pressing a soft kiss to my palm.

"I'm fine." He answers my questioning look. "In fact, I've never felt better."

I laugh, even though it hurts. "We're quite a pair. Aren't we?"

He nods. "I would do it again, angel. For you I would do anything."

I open my mouth to speak, but the words catch in my throat.

He kisses my palm again. "I know why you didn't tell me the truth. You felt it was your only choice. But know this, Evangeline. You can trust me. You need not put yourself in danger for my sake. Not now or ever again."

I peek over his shoulder to the three people standing outside the door, and despite my blurred vision from the eye still swollen shut, I recognize them all—the king, the heir apparent and his wife.

"Did you really mean what you said to your father, or was I still out?" I ask, not sure I'll be able to take his answer either way. If I dreamed it, it means I will still lose him in a matter of weeks. If what I heard was real, then Benedict is giving up everything. For me. And I cannot ask him to do that, no matter how much I want him for myself.

I glance the length of my body to see the plaster extending from the bottom of my thigh to my ankle and clench my stomach muscles.

"You're not okay," he says. "But you will be. And I will spend the rest of my days making sure of it."

"But I can't ask you—"

Benedict doesn't let me finish. "You aren't asking. I'm choosing, Evangeline. I choose happiness. And my happiness…is you." He clears his throat. "That is, if you'll have me."

I pull him to me as best I can, kissing him regardless of the pain. Because he is my prince.

"You saved my life," I say against his lips, tasting the salt of our mingled tears.

"And you saved mine right back."

He kisses me with such tenderness, such carefulness, and my heart bursts with a love I never knew could exist.

"I love you, Benedict. God, I love you," I say but then gasp. "I'm sorry. I didn't mean to use the Lord's name in vain."

Benedict leans back and raises a brow. "I am still a man of faith, angel. Always will be. But you are my earthly ruler. My very own heavenly body. I pray to your altar now and expect no apologies from my soul's savior."

"All right. All right," I hear from over Benedict's shoulder. "I've waited long enough. It's time I thank the woman who tempted my brother from the cloth."

"Nikolai!" the princess calls out, following on her husband's heels. "I'm sorry, Benedict," she says from where they stand at the foot of my bed. "You know your brother is impossible." She flashes me a warm smile, and my heart swells at the sight of the future king and his bride, the way he looks upon her with unrivaled adoration.

I swallow hard when my gaze falls on Benedict. Because he gazes at me with that same reverence.

"Tell me, brother," Benedict says as he stands to greet our visitors. "Is it I who should be thanking you? Did you send Evangeline to my tower?"

Nikolai cocks a dark brow and gives his brother a crooked grin. "I did call The Jewel Box, yes. Does your lady love go by the name of Pearl? I called on an old friend for a little favor."

"Pearl?" Benedict says with a tone that makes me feel like I'm missing some private joke. "No. The Madam gave Evangeline the name Ruby, but no one will ever call her that again."

Nikolai crosses his arms. "Fair enough." Then his eyes fall on mine. "Benedict and X have filled me in on your family's history. I am sorry for all you've suffered in the name of your father's legacy. The kingdom is indebted to the work he did—to the work your brother will continue."

I nod. "And I, as well," I say.

"What?" Benedict asks, his eyes wide.

"I'm an artist," I say. "I want to use my talent to further protect the kingdom. I'm not saying I want to join The Order. But I want to help in any way I can."

The king steps forward and bows his head. "It

seems I was quick to judge. Please accept my deepest gratitude, Evangeline."

"Thank you, Your Highness," I say.

X strides up behind the king, his sons and the princess. "Actually," he says, "I'm quite impressed with your forgery of the map and the speed with which you produced it. The Order could use someone like you as a friend—in case we ever need such services." He glances toward Benedict. "I swear she will be safe, Your Highness. Any work she might do for us would be highly secure and confidential. Though the Madam will not be able to harm you, Evangeline, Nightgardin still seeks the Spring and will try again to find the map. And if she relayed to her employers what your brother said in his unconscious babblings…"

"By the light of the moon, Evangeline," I say. "You know what that means?"

X walks to the window on the opposite side of my bed, pulling open the shade with a gloved hand. It is not yet dawn. He takes a map from beneath his arm—one I know immediately is the real deal—unrolls it and holds it up to the moonlight. The only sound is a collective gasp as we all peer at an image coming into view, an illustration superimposed over the map of the catacombs. It looks an awful lot like a small body of water—the Spring.

As quickly as he shows us the moonlit image, X clears his throat and rolls the map back up.

"Your father's angel kept this map safe for years, and while I trust the palace is the best place to continue hiding it, I will leave it to The Order's discretion. For everyone's safety, the final location will be kept a secret from all but our members."

Everyone nods their agreement.

"Also, Miss Evangeline, Jasper is awake and asking for you. I've already sent for his wife and daughter to travel from their safe house."

New tears spring from my eyes as I look to Benedict, my love.

"Take me to him. Please."

He nods. "I'll have a nurse come with a wheelchair." He turns to X and his family. "Can we have a moment alone?" he asks.

With that, the whole party bows their heads and takes their leave.

And then my prince takes my hand once more—and drops to his knees beside my bed.

CHAPTER TWENTY

Benedict

"BENEDICT, WHAT ARE you doing?" Evangeline asks in a stunned voice.

"Angel, you have brought me to my knees," I say simply. "My entire life I have walked about with a sense that something was missing inside me. For a long time I had hoped that joining the church would bring me that sense of purpose, but I was wrong. While I will always have a strong faith, I know now that what was missing was you."

Her eyes fill with tears and shine with such love that for a moment I am unable to speak. Finally, I clear my throat and move on.

"You are my soul's mate, Evangeline. My darling. My forever. And I don't want to waste another second not giving you everything your heart might desire. I am nothing but a second son, with no hope of inheriting our kingdom's ancient throne, but I will devote my existence from this moment forward to giving you the happily-ever-after that you deserve."

"What are you saying?" Her voice cracks.

Even in this hospital bed, after all those monsters did, the sight of her takes my breath away.

Carefully, I engulf her hand in my own. "I am saying that I love you. And you would make me the happiest of men if you'd be willing to take me as your husband."

She gasps. *Marriage.* Her lips form the word, but no sound escapes.

I incline my head. "I wasn't quite prepared today. I don't have a ring, but we can get one made, any type of stone, any setting, you say the word and it's good as—"

"Yes!" She pushes herself into a half-sit, tossing her head, her hair pouring over one shoulder like a waterfall of golden silk. "Yes, a million times over."

I let out a shaky breath. I have chosen, just like my mother said I should. I have chosen happiness. But I will still do good—by this woman and by all who shall cross our path. Because she is goodness incarnate, and in her angelic light I shall not stray.

"You mean it?" I ask.

She giggles. "Don't look so shocked. Have you looked in a mirror? Loving that face for the rest of my life isn't exactly going to be a hardship." She presses a palm over my heart. "And loving this?" she says with a reverence I'm not expecting. "It's not within my power to do otherwise."

I rise up and kiss her softly, given her bruised and battered state. My lips brush hers, and as I move to pull away, she reaches out and grabs my head, pressing my mouth firmly to hers. When her sweet tongue tangles with mine, I growl with repressed desire. She tastes like peaches and brown sugar. I want to devour her but first must get her well.

And that is exactly what I do. For the next two weeks, I spend every waking second in the hospital as she recuperates behind the safety of The Order. We're still trying to sort out the breach within our guard—how Gideon came into royal employ and if there are others such as him within our midst. During the periods when Evangeline rests, I stand watch with the brethren. When she tends to personal needs or is taken for therapy, I wander the wards. Mix with the people. See the operations of this remarkable institution, the dedication of the doctors, nurses and other staff.

"You are wonderful with the children," I tell her one evening after watching my love, from her wheel-chair, teach a painting class in the pediatric wing. "You are everyone's angel, it seems."

She slides over in her bed, patting the spot beside her, and I crawl in to cradle her healing body like I've done so many nights before.

"I told you," she says. "I want to give back. I always thought my art didn't mean anything to anyone but me, but I can help The Order. I can help these kids." Her eyes shine with the happiest of tears. "I never thought I could make a difference, but—"

I silence her with a soft kiss, and she melts into me.

"Everyone you touch, angel, is better for it. Don't you see that?"

She sniffles and smiles. "I think I'm starting to," she says.

"What if we can make a difference together?" I ask, and her brows furrow. "I've been invited to serve on the board of directors. The royal family will be contributing a sizable donation to spearhead a campaign to build a specialty hospital just for children. The vote has been finalized, and it seems the board has accepted my proposal for what to call it." Her eyes widen. "The Giuseppe Vernazza Hospital for Children."

I was wrong. The tears that stream down her face, these are the happiest I've seen, though I know this moment is bittersweet. If I could give Evangeline her father back, I would. Instead, I will see to it that we honor his name with work that will take care of our future generations.

"Oh, Benedict," she says, and I kiss her sweetly on the forehead. "I didn't think it was possible to love you more than I already do, but you keep surprising me. Ever since Jasper, Camille and Lola went into hiding, I've felt so lost without them. If not for you, I don't know how I would have survived their departure. You are my family now, and you've given our future such purpose. I don't know how I could be happier."

I pull her close and breathe in the sweet scent of her. "This is only the beginning, angel. There is so much more to come."

At last the day Evangeline is to leave arrives. I find her in her hospital room, sitting in a chair by the window.

"All set?" I ask.

"Yes, but we have to wait another hour," she says with a pretty pout.

"Why?"

I am the prince. If my future princess is ready to leave, there should be a team of porters assembled to cater to her whim.

"Because X said that he had to talk to you and Nikolai together."

She runs a hand over my chest. "We have sixty whole minutes to kill. Whatever shall we do to pass the time?"

There's no mistaking the naughty tease to her tone. My cock strains against my pants. I have been so focused on her healing that for weeks we have not been able to connect in such a way that acknowledges our simmering chemistry.

But now our attraction is bubbling over.

"Are you sure?" I murmur, bracing her face between my hands.

She licks her lips and then, grabbing my wrist, lowers her mouth over my index finger, sucking it hard. When she reaches my knuckle, she gives a gentle wink.

"Fuck me hard," I rumble.

"Gladly," she purrs. "Lock the door, my liege."

Because when I give her this, the most intimate part of me, I am not just giving her my body and heart. She owns my soul.

Evangeline

This is my future. This man who is finally able to see his true potential. This man who never thought his life was his own choice, yet once he realized it was…he chose me.

"I love you, my prince," I say as I sink over him again, burying every inch inside me yet never feeling like I can truly get enough.

"And I love you, my angel. My soul's keeper. My Evangeline."

He kisses me, then tilts his head to offer me a wicked grin. This man is so full of goodness, but, oh, how I love it when he's bad.

"What?" I ask, and he answers by slipping his hand between us, spreading my slick, wet heat over my swollen clit.

I cry out, but he whispers a soft "Shh. Remember where we are. You don't want the nurses thinking you need help. Do you?"

I shake my head, then bite my lip to keep from making another sound.

"And there will be reporters waiting for our exit. Everyone wants to catch a glimpse of Edenvale's newest princess-to-be." His words are measured and calm, but I can tell he's barely keeping it together. Just to test him, I clench my inner muscles around his cock, and he hisses through his teeth.

I raise my brows in silent victory, but all he does is grin.

"I'm going to make you come now, angel. I'm going to make you come so fucking hard, so do what you have to do so as not to give us away."

And because I believe him, I nod. Then I bury my face in his neck and bite on his skin, hoping I don't draw blood. Because as I lift my hips, allowing him to slide out slowly, his hand slips between us again so that when he plunges back inside, hitting me precisely where he knows he should, I all but come apart at the seams as the orgasm rocks through my core, both inside and out.

I shudder against him as he growls into my hair, his climax taking its grip, and he finally loses control, savagely crying out like I've never heard him before.

I burst into a fit of giggles, my head still hiding in the crook of his neck.

"Well," I say through sharp pants. "At least the nurses won't think I'm in any danger."

He throws his head back and laughs, my beautiful, wonderful, soul-stealing prince.

And just as predicted, an impatient fist pounds at the door.

Benedict and I clean ourselves up in record time. I seat myself on the side of the hospital bed and smooth out my skirt while he finally unlocks the door.

Nikolai raises a brow and clears his throat.

"What?" Benedict asks, running a hand through hair I notice is dampened with sweat at his nape.

The corner of Nikolai's mouth quirks up. "Nothing, Your Holiness. I just usually wear my clothing with the tags on the inside. And in the back."

That's when I see the stitching on Benedict's pants—because it's on the outside. Inside out and backward does, likely, give us away, and it's all I can do to stifle my laughter.

Benedict simply shrugs. "What can I say?" he asks. "Evangeline gets to go home today. To *our* home. We decided to celebrate early."

Nikolai looks at me and winks, and my cheeks turn red-hot.

"Well," Nikolai says, "fix yourself up, because X will be here any minute. I'd like to know why I was summoned when I should be home ravishing my own wife. Again."

Benedict drops his pants right then and there, turning them the way they should be before pulling them on again.

"Really?" he says to his older brother. "We're going to take sibling rivalry to this level? Because I've got decades of virginity to make up for. I don't think you could keep up, old man."

"Boys," I say, and they turn their attention to me. "As much as I'm enjoying this little cock fight…" I nod toward the door, where X stands in one of his impeccably tailored suits. Sometimes I wonder what goes on when he's not saving our lives. Actually, no. I always wonder. As much as X has opened my eyes these past months, so much about him, The Order and my family's history is still a mystery.

"Come with me" is all he says.

"I'm not leaving Evangeline," Benedict tells him. "She's not yet been released."

X nods. "We are not leaving hospital grounds. Bring her, as well. This will affect her life, too."

Benedict reaches for my hand, and Nikolai's playful smile disappears. Both men follow their guard with measured calm, but the way Benedict squeezes my hand tells me of his unspoken fear. What are we about to walk into?

X guides us to an elevator, where we ride up several floors to the intensive care unit. I swallow hard.

This is where Jasper was before he came out of his coma. I breathe deeply, and it's as if X reads my mind.

"Your brother and his family are safely hidden, Evangeline. This…is something new."

The doors open to the quiet floor. We pass the nurses' station and travel down the hall until its very end. Room 7104.

The door is cracked, but we cannot see inside.

"What is this, X?" Benedict asks, but X just holds a finger to his lips.

We listen to the murmurings going on inside.

"He's lost consciousness again," a female voice says. "But he was awake long enough for me to get some answers. His name, which we will have to verify by calling the family, and enough evidence for me to conclude this is quite the traumatic brain injury."

"What do you mean?" a deep male voice asks.

"Doctor, our patient has no idea how he ended up in Edenvale. When I asked him to recall the most recent national event he'd seen reported on the news— he spoke of a tabloid headline concerning Prince Nikolai's sexual exploits upon a French heiress's yacht."

Benedict gives his brother a knowing stare.

"Hey," Nikolai says. "While I do remember that exploit fondly, that was the old me. I exploit no one other than my wife now." He quirks a brow.

"What's the matter with that?" we hear the male doctor ask.

The woman clears her throat. "Sir, the headline is just over a year old. If the last thing he remembers is a story about his brother, our patient seems to have lost a year of his life."

"Brother?" Benedict says, his palm damp against my own hand. "X, what the hell is she talking about?"

X steps back as the door flies open, startling the man and woman in white lab coats.

Finally, I see a young man lying in bed, his face bruised and swollen, a strip of gauze taped over what must be a gash on his left temple and the telltale scar down the side of a face as famous as his brothers, who stand before me.

"What the fuck is he doing here?" Nikolai asks.

"So it's true," the female doctor says.

Benedict nods.

"Benedict?" I ask. "Is that really…?"

He pulls me close and squeezes me to his side, as if I am the only thing grounding him right now.

"Yes. That's Damien," he says softly. "Edenvale's banished prince. Our brother."

X finally lets out a breath. "I don't think it's a coincidence he was found the same day Evangeline is set to be released. This is a message from Nightgardin. It seems they will use any means to gain the location of the Spring."

EPILOGUE

X

IT'S BEEN A fucking day—escorting the royal family back to the palace. All the family. Even Damien, the youngest of the Lorentz brothers and no longer a complete persona non grata, is in the palace for the first time in years since betraying his eldest brother, Nikolai, by first seducing his fiancée—and then causing the accident that took her life and scarred him forever. He bears not only a spiritual stain…but the physical reminders, as well.

I have more business to get through, but as I park my bike in front of The Jewel Box, Rosegate's finest brothel once more now that the Madam is gone, I smile at the thought of mixing in a little pleasure first.

A window slides open at the entrance, and I show my lifetime pass. The door clicks open, and I stride inside, barely noticing the sumptuous red velvet furniture, the golden wallpaper or the runway-caliber women sauntering about wearing nothing but the jewels for which they are named. With Benedict being her one and only client, Ruby—or Evangeline—never worked the floor, never bore the jeweled mark of her trade. She was not meant for this line of work, and for her I am happy that with His Highness she found something more fitting. But the women here now— they are consummate professionals, more than adept in their skill. And they take pleasure in their craft.

I see Diamond, Amethyst and Topaz. Emerald is leading a patron up the stairs by his tie. Opal is putting on an old-fashioned burlesque show on a small stage in the room to my right. A trio of Danish businessmen stare in rapt attention.

But my Pearl is waiting for me on the third floor, in a room designed to look like the sea. I climb the stairs with slow purpose, my cock stirring in anticipation.

It's been too long.

The door to her bedchamber isn't latched, so I push it open—and frown. The giant oyster-shaped bed is empty. Instead, there is a Bluetooth earpiece resting in the center of an overstuffed pillow.

Shit.

Looks like business is coming first.

I hate it when that happens.

I pop in the earpiece. "White Knight is in the castle," I say, using the old code name for Damien.

"They're saying amnesia," the husky female voice answers in my ear. "Is it real or an act?"

"Hard to say." I cross my arms. "Seems legitimate, but we've seen good actors before."

"This would be just the sort of diabolical ruse Nightgardin would attempt to try to gain access to the Spring. Corrupt one of our own, and turn him into a plant to betray us from the inside."

"Or he really has lost his memory."

"Figure it out," she snaps. The line goes dead.

"Good night to you, too," I say wryly, removing the earpiece and throwing it out the open window. It self-destructs before it hits the ground in a staccato crack, like a car backfiring.

I don't take it personally. The Order prides itself on absolute focus on the mission to prevent a cataclysmic world war over the Spring. But we're all human. Even her, once my protégé and now my boss.

We all have feelings.

The floor creaks behind me, and suddenly I am having a hell of a lot of feelings. I turn to find Pearl dressed like Holly Golightly from *Breakfast at Tiffany's* right down to the cigarette holder, little black dress and pearl choker.

She knows she's killing me slowly.

"You done with work yet?" She pouts. "Not very nice, kicking a girl out of her room."

"Sorry, babe," I say. "You wouldn't believe the day that I've had."

She drops the cigarette holder and crushes the ember with the toe of her stiletto before undoing her dress. It falls to the ground, and my cock responds with unbridled need.

Even my self-control has limits.

She stands with her legs spread, wearing fucking garters, and I spy a small wet spot in the apex of her sheer thong.

"Forget about saving the world tonight." She kneads her breasts in the push-up bra. "Let me save you for once."

"From what?" I lick my lips. Ready for the feast ahead.

She arches a brow and drops her gaze to the giant erection in my suit pants. "Yourself."

* * * * *

COMING SOON!

We really hope you enjoyed reading this book. If you're looking for more romance, be sure to head to the shops when new books are available on

Thursday
28th June

To see which titles are coming soon, please visit
millsandboon.co.uk

LET'S TALK
Romance

For exclusive extracts, competitions
and special offers, find us online:

f facebook.com/millsandboon

📷 @millsandboonuk

🐦 @millsandboon

Or get in touch on 0844 844 1351*

For all the latest titles coming soon, visit
millsandboon.co.uk/nextmonth